TALES

— of —

JAPAN

TALES
— of —
JAPAN

*Traditional Stories of
Monsters and Magic*

ILLUSTRATIONS BY
Kotaro Chiba

CHRONICLE BOOKS
SAN FRANCISCO

Illustrations by Kotaro Chiba, copyright © 2019 by Chronicle Books.

Library of Congress Cataloging-in-Publication Data:
Names: Chiba, Kotaro, illustrator.
Title: Tales of Japan : traditional stories of monsters and magic /
    illustrations by Kotaro Chiba.
Description: San Francisco, California : Chronicle Books LLC, [2019]
Identifiers: LCCN 2018016472 | ISBN 9781452174464 hardcover : alk. paper
Subjects: LCSH: Tales—Japan. | Folklore—Japan. | Mythology, Japanese.
Classification: LCC GR340 .T325 2019 | DDC 398.20952—dc23 LC record available at
https://lccn.loc.gov/2018016472

Manufactured in China.

Designed by Lizzie Vaughan
Series Design by Emily Dubin
Typeset in Adobe Caslon, Lydian, and Majorelle.

10 9 8 7 6

Chronicle books and gifts are available at special quantity discounts to corporations,
professional associations, literacy programs, and other organizations.
For details and discount information, please contact our premiums department at
corporatesales@chroniclebooks.com or at 1-800-759-0190.

Chronicle Books LLC
680 Second Street
San Francisco, California 94107
www.chroniclebooks.com

"'Akinosuké must have been dreaming,'
one of them exclaimed, with a laugh.
'What did you see, Akinosuké, that was strange?'"

—LAFCADIO HEARN,
"The Dream of Akinosuké"

CONTENTS

—

JOURNEYS 8

The Dream of Akinosuké 10

The Jelly Fish and the Monkey 18

Momotaro, or the Story of the Son of a Peach 28

The Happy Hunter and the Skillful Fisher 42

The Bamboo-Cutter and the Moon-Child 60

GHOSTS AND MONSTERS 76

The Story of Mimi-Nashi-Hōïchi 78

Yuki-Onna 90

Diplomacy 96

Mujina 100

A Dead Secret 104

Rokuro-Kubi 108

JUSTICE 120

The Tongue-Cut Sparrow 122

The Farmer and the Badger 132

The Story of the Old Man Who Made
Withered Trees to Flower 140

The Mirror of Matsuyama 150

SOURCES 166

JOURNEYS

THE DREAM
of AKINOSUKÉ

I n the district called Toichi of Yamato province, there used to live
a gōshi named Miyata Akinosuké . . . [Here I must tell you that in
Japanese feudal times there was a privileged class of soldier-farmers,
—free-holders,—corresponding to the class of yeomen in England; and
these were called gōshi.]

In Akinosuké's garden there was a great and ancient cedar-tree, under
which he was wont to rest on sultry days. One very warm afternoon he
was sitting under this tree with two of his friends, fellow-gōshi, chatting
and drinking wine, when he felt all of a sudden very drowsy,—so drowsy
that he begged his friends to excuse him for taking a nap in their presence.
Then he lay down at the foot of the tree, and dreamed this dream:—

He thought that as he was lying there in his garden, he saw a procession, like the train of some great daimyō, descending a hill near by, and
that he got up to look at it. A very grand procession it proved to be,—more
imposing than anything of the kind which he had ever seen before; and it
was advancing toward his dwelling. He observed in the van of it a number of young men richly appareled, who were drawing a great lacquered
palace-carriage, or gosho-guruma, hung with bright blue silk. When the
procession arrived within a short distance of the house it halted; and a richly
dressed man—evidently a person of rank—advanced from it, approached

Akinosuké, bowed to him profoundly, and then said:—

"Honored Sir, you see before you a kérai [vassal] of the Kokuō of Tokoyo.[1] My master, the King, commands me to greet you in his august name, and to place myself wholly at your disposal. He also bids me inform you that he augustly desires your presence at the palace. Be therefore pleased immediately to enter this honorable carriage, which he has sent for your conveyance."

Upon hearing these words Akinosuké wanted to make some fitting reply; but he was too much astonished and embarrassed for speech;—and in the same moment his will seemed to melt away from him, so that he could only do as the kérai bade him. He entered the carriage; the kérai took a place beside him, and made a signal; the drawers, seizing the silken ropes, turned the great vehicle southward;—and the journey began.

In a very short time, to Akinosuké's amazement, the carriage stopped in front of a huge two-storied gateway (rōmon), of a Chinese style, which he had never before seen. Here the kérai dismounted, saying, "I go to announce the honorable arrival,"—and he disappeared. After some little waiting, Akinosuké saw two noble-looking men, wearing robes of purple silk and high caps of the form indicating lofty rank, come from the gateway. These, after having respectfully saluted him, helped him to descend from the carriage, and led him through the great gate and across a vast garden, to the entrance of a palace whose front appeared to extend, west and east, to a distance of miles. Akinosuké was then shown into a reception-room of wonderful size and splendor. His guides conducted him to the place of honor, and respectfully seated themselves apart; while serving-maids, in costume of ceremony, brought refreshments. When

---

1. This name "Tokoyo" is indefinite. According to circumstances it may signify any unknown country,—or that undiscovered country from whose bourn no traveler returns,—or that Fairyland of far-eastern fable, the Realm of Hōrai. The term "Kokuō" means the ruler of a country,— therefore a king. The original phrase, *Tokoyo no Kokuō*, might be rendered here as "the Ruler of Hōrai," or "the King of Fairyland."

Akinosuké had partaken of the refreshments, the two purple-robed attendants bowed low before him, and addressed him in the following words,—each speaking alternately, according to the etiquette of courts:—

"It is now our honorable duty to inform you . . . as to the reason of your having been summoned hither . . . Our master, the King, augustly desires that you become his son-in-law; . . . and it is his wish and command that you shall wed this very day . . . the August Princess, his maiden-daughter . . . We shall soon conduct you to the presence-chamber . . . where His Augustness even now is waiting to receive you . . . But it will be necessary that we first invest you . . . with the appropriate garments of ceremony."[2]

Having thus spoken, the attendants rose together, and proceeded to an alcove containing a great chest of gold lacquer. They opened the chest, and took from it various robes and girdles of rich material, and a kamuri, or regal headdress. With these they attired Akinosuké as befitted a princely bridegroom; and he was then conducted to the presence-room, where he saw the Kokuō of Tokoyo seated upon the daiza,[3] wearing a high black cap of state, and robed in robes of yellow silk. Before the daiza, to left and right, a multitude of dignitaries sat in rank, motionless and splendid as images in a temple; and Akinosuké, advancing into their midst, saluted the king with the triple prostration of usage. The king greeted him with gracious words, and then said:—

"You have already been informed as to the reason of your having been summoned to Our presence. We have decided that you shall become the adopted husband of Our only daughter;—and the wedding ceremony shall now be performed."

---

2.   The last phrase, according to old custom, had to be uttered by both attendants at the same time. All these ceremonial observances can still be studied on the Japanese stage.

3.   This was the name given to the estrade, or dais, upon which a feudal prince or ruler sat in state. The term literally signifies "great seat."

As the king finished speaking, a sound of joyful music was heard; and a long train of beautiful court ladies advanced from behind a curtain, to conduct Akinosuké to the room in which his bride awaited him.

The room was immense; but it could scarcely contain the multitude of guests assembled to witness the wedding ceremony. All bowed down before Akinosuké as he took his place, facing the King's daughter, on the kneeling-cushion prepared for him. As a maiden of heaven the bride appeared to be; and her robes were beautiful as a summer sky. And the marriage was performed amid great rejoicing.

Afterwards the pair were conducted to a suite of apartments that had been prepared for them in another portion of the palace; and there they received the congratulations of many noble persons, and wedding gifts beyond counting.

SOME DAYS LATER Akinosuké was again summoned to the throne-room. On this occasion he was received even more graciously than before; and the King said to him:—

"In the southwestern part of Our dominion there is an island called Raishū. We have now appointed you Governor of that island. You will find the people loyal and docile; but their laws have not yet been brought into proper accord with the laws of Tokoyo; and their customs have not been properly regulated. We entrust you with the duty of improving their social condition as far as may be possible; and We desire that you shall rule them with kindness and wisdom. All preparations necessary for your journey to Raishū have already been made."

SO AKINOSUKÉ and his bride departed from the palace of Tokoyo, accompanied to the shore by a great escort of nobles and officials; and they embarked upon a ship of state provided by the king. And with favoring winds they safely sailed to Raishū, and found the good people of that island assembled upon the beach to welcome them.

AKINOSUKÉ ENTERED AT ONCE upon his new duties; and they did not prove to be hard. During the first three years of his governorship he was occupied chiefly with the framing and the enactment of laws; but he had wise counselors to help him, and he never found the work unpleasant. When it was all finished, he had no active duties to perform, beyond attending the rites and ceremonies ordained by ancient custom. The country was so healthy and so fertile that sickness and want were unknown; and the people were so good that no laws were ever broken. And Akinosuké dwelt and ruled in Raishū for twenty years more,—making in all twenty-three years of sojourn, during which no shadow of sorrow traversed his life.

But in the twenty-fourth year of his governorship, a great misfortune came upon him; for his wife, who had borne him seven children,—five boys and two girls,—fell sick and died. She was buried, with high pomp, on the summit of a beautiful hill in the district of Hanryōkō; and a monument, exceedingly splendid, was placed upon her grave. But Akinosuké felt such grief at her death that he no longer cared to live.

NOW WHEN THE LEGAL period of mourning was over, there came to Raishū, from the Tokoyo palace, a shisha, or royal messenger. The shisha delivered to Akinosuké a message of condolence, and then said to him:—

"These are the words which our august master, the King of Tokoyo, commands that I repeat to you: 'We will now send you back to your own people and country. As for the seven children, they are the grandsons and granddaughters of the King, and shall be fitly cared for. Do not, therefore, allow your mind to be troubled concerning them.'"

On receiving this mandate, Akinosuké submissively prepared for his departure. When all his affairs had been settled, and the ceremony of bidding farewell to his counselors and trusted officials had been concluded, he was escorted with much honor to the port. There he embarked upon the ship sent for him; and the ship sailed out into the blue sea, under the blue sky; and the shape of the island of Raishū itself turned blue, and then turned grey, and then vanished forever . . . And Akinosuké suddenly awoke—under the cedar-tree in his own garden! . . .

For a moment he was stupefied and dazed. But he perceived his two friends still seated near him,—drinking and chatting merrily. He stared at them in a bewildered way, and cried aloud,—

"How strange!"

"Akinosuké must have been dreaming," one of them exclaimed, with a laugh. "What did you see, Akinosuké, that was strange?"

Then Akinosuké told his dream,—that dream of three-and-twenty years' sojourn in the realm of Tokoyo, in the island of Raishū;—and they were astonished, because he had really slept for no more than a few minutes.

One gōshi said:—

"Indeed, you saw strange things. We also saw something strange while you were napping. A little yellow butterfly was fluttering over your face for a moment or two; and we watched it. Then it alighted on the ground beside you, close to the tree; and almost as soon as it alighted there, a big, big ant came out of a hole and seized it and pulled it down into the hole. Just before you woke up, we saw that very butterfly come out of the hole again, and flutter over your face as before. And then it suddenly disappeared: we do not know where it went."

"Perhaps it was Akinosuké's soul," the other gōshi said;—"certainly I thought I saw it fly into his mouth . . . But, even if that butterfly was Akinosuké's soul, the fact would not explain his dream."

"The ants might explain it," returned the first speaker. "Ants are queer beings—possibly goblins . . . Anyhow, there is a big ant's nest under that cedar-tree." . . .

"Let us look!" cried Akinosuké, greatly moved by this suggestion. And he went for a spade.

THE GROUND ABOUT AND BENEATH the cedar-tree proved to have been excavated, in a most surprising way, by a prodigious colony of ants. The ants had furthermore built inside their excavations; and their tiny constructions of straw, clay, and stems bore an odd resemblance to miniature towns. In the middle of a structure considerably larger than the rest there was a marvelous swarming of small ants around the body of one very big ant, which had yellowish wings and a long black head.

"Why, there is the King of my dream!" cried Akinosuké; "and there is the palace of Tokoyo! . . . How extraordinary! . . . Raishū ought to lie somewhere southwest of it—to the left of that big root . . . Yes!—here it is! . . . How very strange! Now I am sure that I can find the mountain of Hanryōkō, and the grave of the princess." . . .

In the wreck of the nest he searched and searched, and at last discovered a tiny mound, on the top of which was fixed a water-worn pebble, in shape resembling a Buddhist monument. Underneath it he found—embedded in clay—the dead body of a female ant.

THE JELLY FISH
and the MONKEY

L ong, long ago, in old Japan, the Kingdom of the Sea was governed by a wonderful King. He was called Rin Jin, or the Dragon King of the Sea. His power was immense, for he was the ruler of all sea creatures both great and small, and in his keeping were the Jewels of the Ebb and Flow of the Tide. The Jewel of the Ebbing Tide when thrown into the ocean caused the sea to recede from the land, and the Jewel of the Flowing Tide made the waves to rise mountains high and to flow in upon the shore like a tidal wave.

The Palace of Rin Jin was at the bottom of the sea, and was so beautiful that no one has ever seen anything like it even in dreams. The walls were of coral, the roof of jadestone and chrysoprase, and the floors were of the finest mother-of-pearl. But the Dragon King, in spite of his wide-spreading Kingdom, his beautiful Palace and all its wonders, and his power which none disputed throughout the whole sea, was not at all happy, for he reigned alone. At last he thought that if he married he would not only be happier, but also more powerful. So he decided to take a wife. Calling all his fish retainers together, he chose several of them as ambassadors to go through the sea and seek for a young Dragon Princess who would be his bride.

At last they returned to the Palace bringing with them a lovely young dragon. Her scales were of glittering green like the wings of summer beetles, her eyes threw out glances of fire, and she was dressed in gorgeous robes. All the jewels of the sea worked in with embroidery adorned them.

The King fell in love with her at once, and the wedding ceremony was celebrated with great splendor. Every living thing in the sea, from the great whales down to the little shrimps, came in shoals to offer their congratulations to the bride and bridegroom and to wish them a long and prosperous life. Never had there been such an assemblage or such gay festivities in the Fish-World before. The train of bearers who carried the bride's possessions to her new home seemed to reach across the waves from one end of the sea to the other. Each fish carried a phosphorescent lantern and was dressed in ceremonial robes, gleaming blue and pink and silver; and the waves as they rose and fell and broke that night seemed to be rolling masses of white and green fire, for the phosphorus shone with double brilliancy in honor of the event.

Now for a time the Dragon King and his bride lived very happily. They loved each other dearly, and the bridegroom day after day took delight in showing his bride all the wonders and treasures of his coral Palace, and she was never tired of wandering with him through its vast halls and gardens. Life seemed to them both like a long summer's day.

Two months passed in this happy way, and then the Dragon Queen fell ill and was obliged to stay in bed. The King was sorely troubled when he saw his precious bride so ill, and at once sent for the fish doctor to come and give her some medicine. He gave special orders to the servants to nurse her carefully and to wait upon her with diligence, but in spite of all the nurses' assiduous care and the medicine that the doctor prescribed, the young Queen showed no signs of recovery, but grew daily worse.

Then the Dragon King interviewed the doctor and blamed him for not curing the Queen. The doctor was alarmed at Rin Jin's evident displeasure, and excused his want of skill by saying that although he knew the right kind of medicine to give the invalid, it was impossible to find it in the sea.

"Do you mean to tell me that you can't get the medicine here?" asked the Dragon King.

"It is just as you say!" said the doctor.

"Tell me what it is you want for the Queen," demanded Rin Jin.

"I want the liver of a live monkey!" answered the doctor.

"The liver of a live monkey! Of course that will be most difficult to get," said the King.

"If we could only get that for the Queen, Her Majesty would soon recover," said the doctor.

"Very well, that decides it; we must get it somehow or other. But where are we most likely to find a monkey?" asked the King.

Then the doctor told the Dragon King that some distance to the south there was a Monkey Island where a great many monkeys lived.

"If only you could capture one of these monkeys," said the doctor.

"How can any of my people capture a monkey?" said the Dragon King, greatly puzzled. "The monkeys live on dry land, while we live in the water; and out of our element we are quite powerless! I don't see what we can do!"

"That has been my difficulty too," said the doctor. "But amongst your innumerable servants you surely can find one who can go on shore for that express purpose!"

"Something must be done," said the King, and calling his chief steward he consulted him on the matter.

The chief steward thought for some time, and then, as if struck by a sudden thought, said joyfully:

"I know what we must do! There is the *kurage* (jelly fish). He is certainly ugly to look at, but he is proud of being able to walk on land with his four legs like a tortoise. Let us send him to the Island of Monkeys to catch one."

The jelly fish was then summoned to the King's presence, and was told by His Majesty what was required of him.

The jelly fish, on being told of the unexpected mission which was to be entrusted to him, looked very troubled, and said that he had never been to the island in question, and as he had never had any experience in catching monkeys he was afraid that he would not be able to get one.

"Well," said the chief steward, "if you depend on your strength or dexterity you will never catch a monkey. The only way is to play a trick on one!"

"How can I play a trick on a monkey? I don't know how to do it," said the perplexed jelly fish.

"This is what you must do," said the wily chief steward. "When you approach the Island of Monkeys and meet some of them, you must try to get very friendly with one. Tell him that you are a servant of the Dragon King, and invite him to come and visit you and see the Dragon King's Palace. Try and describe to him as vividly as you can the grandeur of the Palace and the wonders of the sea so as to arouse his curiosity and make him long to see it all!"

"But how am I to get the monkey here? You know monkeys don't swim," said the reluctant jelly fish.

"You must carry him on your back. What is the use of your shell if you can't do that!" said the chief steward.

"Won't he be very heavy?" queried *kurage* again.

"You mustn't mind that, for you are working for the Dragon King," replied the chief steward.

"I will do my best then," said the jelly fish, and he swam away from the Palace and started off towards the Monkey Island. Swimming swiftly he reached his destination in a few hours, and landed by a convenient wave upon the shore. On looking round he saw not far away a big pine-tree with drooping branches and on one of those branches was just what he was looking for—a live monkey.

"I'm in luck!" thought the jelly fish. "Now I must flatter the creature and try to entice him to come back with me to the Palace, and my part will be done!"

So the jelly fish slowly walked towards the pine-tree. In those ancient days the jelly fish had four legs and a hard shell like a tortoise. When he got to the pine-tree he raised his voice and said:

"How do you do, Mr. Monkey? Isn't it a lovely day?"

"A very fine day," answered the monkey from the tree. "I have never seen you in this part of the world before. Where have you come from and what is your name?"

"My name is kurage or jelly fish. I am one of the servants of the Dragon King. I have heard so much of your beautiful island that I have come on purpose to see it," answered the jelly fish.

"I am very glad to see you," said the monkey.

"By the bye," said the jelly fish, "have you ever seen the Palace of the Dragon King of the Sea where I live?"

"I have often heard of it, but I have never seen it!" answered the monkey.

"Then you ought most surely to come. It is a great pity for you to go through life without seeing it. The beauty of the Palace is beyond all description—it is certainly to my mind the most lovely place in the world," said the jelly fish.

"Is it so beautiful as all that?" asked the monkey in astonishment.

Then the jelly fish saw his chance, and went on describing to the best of his ability the beauty and grandeur of the Sea King's Palace, and the wonders of the garden with its curious trees of white, pink and red coral, and the still more curious fruits like great jewels hanging on the branches. The monkey grew more and more interested, and as he listened he came down the tree step by step so as not to lose a word of the wonderful story.

"I have got him at last!" thought the jelly fish, but aloud he said:

"Mr. Monkey. I must now go back. As you have never seen the Palace of the Dragon King, won't you avail yourself of this splendid opportunity by coming with me? I shall then be able to act as guide and show you all the sights of the sea, which will be even more wonderful to you—a land-lubber."

"I should love to go," said the monkey, "but how am I to cross the water? I can't swim, as you surely know!"

"There is no difficulty about that. I can carry you on my back."

"That will be troubling you too much," said the monkey.

"I can do it quite easily. I am stronger than I look, so you needn't hesitate," said the jelly fish, and taking the monkey on his back he stepped into the sea.

"Keep very still, Mr. Monkey," said the jelly fish. "You mustn't fall into the sea; I am responsible for your safe arrival at the King's Palace."

"Please don't go so fast, or I am sure I shall fall off," said the monkey.

Thus they went along, the jelly fish skimming through the waves with the monkey sitting on his back. When they were about halfway, the jelly fish, who knew very little of anatomy, began to wonder if the monkey had his liver with him or not!

"Mr. Monkey, tell me, have you such a thing as a liver with you?"

The monkey was very much surprised at this queer question, and asked what the jelly fish wanted with a liver.

"That is the most important thing of all," said the stupid jelly fish, "so as soon as I recollected it, I asked you if you had yours with you."

"Why is my liver so important to you?" asked the monkey.

"Oh! you will learn the reason later," said the jelly fish.

The monkey grew more and more curious and suspicious, and urged the jelly fish to tell him for what his liver was wanted, and ended up by appealing to his hearer's feelings by saying that he was very troubled at what he had been told.

Then the jelly fish, seeing how anxious the monkey looked, was sorry for him, and told him everything. How the Dragon Queen had fallen ill, and how the doctor had said that only the liver of a live monkey would cure her, and how the Dragon King had sent him to find one.

"Now I have done as I was told, and as soon as we arrive at the Palace the doctor will want your liver, so I feel sorry for you!" said the silly jelly fish.

The poor monkey was horrified when he learnt all this, and very angry at the trick played upon him. He trembled with fear at the thought of what was in store for him.

But the monkey was a clever animal, and he thought it the wisest plan not to show any sign of the fear he felt, so he tried to calm himself and to think of some way by which he might escape.

"The doctor means to cut me open and then take my liver out! Why I shall die!" thought the monkey. At last a bright thought struck him, so he said quite cheerfully to the jelly fish:

"What a pity it was, Mr. Jelly Fish, that you did not speak of this before we left the island!"

"If I had told why I wanted you to accompany me you would certainly have refused to come," answered the jelly fish.

"You are quite mistaken," said the monkey. "Monkeys can very well spare a liver or two, especially when it is wanted for the Dragon Queen of the Sea. If I had only guessed of what you were in need, I should have presented you with one without waiting to be asked. I have several livers. But the greatest pity is, that as you did not speak in time, I have left all my livers hanging on the pine-tree."

"Have you left your liver behind you?" asked the jelly fish.

"Yes," said the cunning monkey, "during the daytime I usually leave my liver hanging up on the branch of a tree, as it is very much in the way when I am climbing about from tree to tree. To-day, listening to your interesting conversation, I quite forgot it, and left it behind when I came off with you. If only you had spoken in time I should have remembered it, and should have brought it along with me!"

The jelly fish was very disappointed when he heard this, for he believed every word the monkey said. The monkey was of no good without a liver. Finally the jelly fish stopped and told the monkey so.

"Well," said the monkey, "that is soon remedied. I am really sorry to think of all your trouble; but if you will only take me back to the place where you found me, I shall soon be able to get my liver."

The jelly fish did not at all like the idea of going all the way back to the island again; but the monkey assured him that if he would be so kind as to take him back he would get his very best liver, and bring it with him the next time. Thus persuaded, the jelly fish turned his course towards the Monkey Island once more.

No sooner had the jelly fish reached the shore than the sly monkey landed, and getting up into the pine-tree where the jelly fish had first seen him, he cut several capers amongst the branches with joy at being safe home again, and then looking down at the jelly fish said:

"So many thanks for all the trouble you have taken! Please present my compliments to the Dragon King on your return!"

The jelly fish wondered at this speech and the mocking tone in which it was uttered. Then he asked the monkey if it wasn't his intention to come with him at once after getting his liver.

The monkey replied laughingly that he couldn't afford to lose his liver; it was too precious.

"But remember your promise!" pleaded the jelly fish, now very discouraged.

"That promise was false, and anyhow it is now broken!" answered the monkey. Then he began to jeer at the jelly fish and told him that he had been deceiving him the whole time; that he had no wish to lose his life, which he certainly would have done had he gone on to the Sea King's Palace to the old doctor waiting for him, instead of persuading the jelly fish to return under false pretenses.

"Of course, I won't give you my liver, but come and get it if you can!" added the monkey mockingly from the tree.

There was nothing for the jelly fish to do now but to repent of his stupidity, and to return to the Dragon King of the Sea and to confess his failure, so he started sadly and slowly to swim back. The last thing he heard as he glided away, leaving the island behind him, was the monkey laughing at him.

Meanwhile the Dragon King, the doctor, the chief steward, and all the servants were waiting impatiently for the return of the jelly fish. When they caught sight of him approaching the Palace, they hailed him with delight. They began to thank him profusely for all the trouble he had taken in going to Monkey Island, and then they asked him where the monkey was.

Now the day of reckoning had come for the jelly fish. He quaked all over as he told his story. How he had brought the monkey halfway over the sea, and then had stupidly let out the secret of his commission; how the monkey had deceived him by making him believe that he had left his liver behind him.

The Dragon King's wrath was great, and he at once gave orders that the jelly fish was to be severely punished. The punishment was a horrible one. All the bones were to be drawn out from his living body, and he was to be beaten with sticks.

The poor jelly fish, humiliated and horrified beyond all words, cried out for pardon. But the Dragon King's order had to be obeyed. The servants of the Palace forthwith each brought out a stick and surrounded the jelly fish, and after pulling out his bones they beat him to a flat pulp, and then took him out beyond the Palace gates and threw him into the water. Here he was left to suffer and repent his foolish chattering, and to grow accustomed to his new state of bonelessness.

From this story it is evident that in former times the jelly fish once had a shell and bones something like a tortoise, but, ever since the Dragon King's sentence was carried out on the ancestor of the jelly fishes, his descendants have all been soft and boneless just as you see them to-day thrown up by the waves high upon the shores of Japan.

MOMOTARO, or the STORY of the SON of a PEACH

Long, long ago there lived an old man and an old woman; they were peasants, and had to work hard to earn their daily rice. The old man used to go and cut grass for the farmers around, and while he was gone the old woman, his wife, did the work of the house and worked in their own little rice field.

One day the old man went to the hills as usual to cut grass and the old woman took some clothes to the river to wash.

It was nearly summer, and the country was very beautiful to see in its fresh greenness as the two old people went on their way to work. The grass on the banks of the river looked like emerald velvet, and the pussy willows along the edge of the water were shaking out their soft tassels.

The breezes blew and ruffled the smooth surface of the water into wavelets, and passing on touched the cheeks of the old couple who, for some reason they could not explain, felt very happy that morning.

The old woman at last found a nice spot by the river bank and put her basket down. Then she set to work to wash the clothes; she took them one by one out of the basket and washed them in the river and rubbed them on the stones. The water was as clear as crystal, and she could see the tiny fish swimming to and fro, and the pebbles at the bottom.

As she was busy washing her clothes a great peach came bumping down the stream. The old woman looked up from her work and saw this large peach. She was sixty years of age, yet in all her life she had never seen such a big peach as this.

"How delicious that peach must be!" she said to herself. "I must certainly get it and take it home to my old man."

She stretched out her arm to try and get it, but it was quite out of her reach. She looked about for a stick, but there was not one to be seen, and if she went to look for one she would lose the peach.

Stopping a moment to think what she would do, she remembered an old charm-verse. Now she began to clap her hands to keep time to the rolling of the peach down stream, and while she clapped she sang this song:

"Distant water is bitter,
The near water is sweet;
Pass by the distant water
And come into the sweet."

Strange to say, as soon as she began to repeat this little song the peach began to come nearer and nearer the bank where the old woman was standing, till at last it stopped just in front of her so that she was able to take it up in her hands. The old woman was delighted. She could not go on with her work, so happy and excited was she, so she put all the clothes back in her bamboo basket, and with the basket on her back and the peach in her hand she hurried homewards.

It seemed a very long time to her to wait till her husband returned. The old man at last came back as the sun was setting, with a big bundle of grass on his back—so big that he was almost hidden and she could hardly see him. He seemed very tired and used the scythe for a walking stick, leaning on it as he walked along.

As soon as the old woman saw him she called out:

"*O Fii San*! (old man) I have been waiting for you to come home for such a long time to-day!"

"What is the matter? Why are you so impatient?" asked the old man, wondering at her unusual eagerness. "Has anything happened while I have been away?"

"Oh, no!" answered the old woman, "nothing has happened, only I have found a nice present for you!"

"That is good," said the old man. He then washed his feet in a basin of water and stepped up to the veranda.

The old woman now ran into the little room and brought out from the cupboard the big peach. It felt even heavier than before. She held it up to him, saying:

"Just look at this! Did you ever see such a large peach in all your life?"

When the old man looked at the peach he was greatly astonished and said:

"This is indeed the largest peach I have ever seen! Wherever did you buy it?"

"I did not buy it," answered the old woman. "I found it in the river where I was washing." And she told him the whole story.

"I am very glad that you have found it. Let us eat it now, for I am hungry," said the *O Fii San*.

He brought out the kitchen knife, and, placing the peach on a board, was about to cut it when, wonderful to tell, the peach split in two of itself and a clear voice said:

"Wait a bit, old man!" and out stepped a beautiful little child.

The old man and his wife were both so astonished at what they saw that they fell to the ground. The child spoke again:

"Don't be afraid. I am no demon or fairy. I will tell you the truth. Heaven has had compassion on you. Every day and every night you have lamented that you had no child. Your cry has been heard and I am sent to be the son of your old age!"

On hearing this the old man and his wife were very happy. They had cried night and day for sorrow at having no child to help them in their lonely old age, and now that their prayer was answered they were so lost with joy that they did not know where to put their hands or their feet. First the old man took the child up in his arms, and then the old woman did the same; and they named him *Momotaro*, or *Son of a Peach*, because he had come out of a peach.

The years passed quickly by and the child grew to be fifteen years of age. He was taller and far stronger than any other boys of his own age, he had a handsome face and a heart full of courage, and he was very wise for his years. The old couple's pleasure was very great when they looked at him, for he was just what they thought a hero ought to be like.

One day Momotaro came to his foster-father and said solemnly:

"Father, by a strange chance we have become father and son. Your goodness to me has been higher than the mountain grasses which it was your daily work to cut, and deeper than the river where my mother washes the clothes. I do not know how to thank you enough."

"Why," answered the old man, "it is a matter of course that a father should bring up his son. When you are older it will be your turn to take care of us, so after all there will be no profit or loss between us—all will be equal. Indeed, I am rather surprised that you should thank me in this way!" and the old man looked bothered.

"I hope you will be patient with me," said Momotaro; "but before I begin to pay back your goodness to me I have a request to make which I hope you will grant me above everything else."

"I will let you do whatever you wish, for you are quite different to all other boys!"

"Then let me go away at once!"

"What do you say? Do you wish to leave your old father and mother and go away from your old home?"

"I will surely come back again, if you let me go now!"

"Where are you going?"

"You must think it strange that I want to go away," said Momotaro, "because I have not yet told you my reason. Far away from here to the northeast of Japan there is an island in the sea. This island is the stronghold of a band of devils. I have often heard how they invade this land, kill and rob the people, and carry off all they can find. They are not only very wicked but they are disloyal to our Emperor and disobey his laws. They are also cannibals, for they kill and eat some of the poor people who are so unfortunate as to fall into their hands. These devils are very hateful beings. I must go and conquer them and bring back all the plunder of which they have robbed this land. It is for this reason that I want to go away for a short time!"

The old man was much surprised at hearing all this from a mere boy of fifteen. He thought it best to let the boy go. He was strong and fearless, and besides all this, the old man knew he was no common child, for he had been sent to them as a gift from Heaven, and he felt quite sure that the devils would be powerless to harm him.

"All you say is very interesting, Momotaro," said the old man. "I will not hinder you in your determination. You may go if you wish. Go to the island as soon as ever you like and destroy the demons and bring peace to the land."

"Thank you, for all your kindness," said Momotaro, who began to get ready to go that very day. He was full of courage and did not know what fear was.

The old man and woman at once set to work to pound rice in the kitchen mortar to make cakes for Momotaro to take with him on his journey.

At last the cakes were made and Momotaro was ready to start on his long journey.

Parting is always sad. So it was now. The eyes of the two old people were filled with tears and their voices trembled as they said:

"Go with all care and speed. We expect you back victorious!"

Momotaro was very sorry to leave his old parents (though he knew he was coming back as soon as he could), for he thought of how lonely they would be while he was away. But he said "Good-by!" quite bravely.

"I am going now. Take good care of yourselves while I am away. Good-by!" And he stepped quickly out of the house. In silence the eyes of Momotaro and his parents met in farewell.

Momotaro now hurried on his way till it was midday. He began to feel hungry, so he opened his bag and took out one of the rice-cakes and sat down under a tree by the side of the road to eat it. While he was thus having his lunch a dog almost as large as a colt came running out from the high grass. He made straight for Momotaro, and showing his teeth, said in a fierce way:

"You are a rude man to pass my field without asking permission first. If you leave me all the cakes you have in your bag you may go; otherwise I will bite you till I kill you!"

Momotaro only laughed scornfully:

"What is that you are saying? Do you know who I am? I am Momotaro, and I am on my way to subdue the devils in their island stronghold in the northeast of Japan. If you try to stop me on my way there I will cut you in two from the head downwards!"

The dog's manner at once changed. His tail dropped between his legs, and coming near he bowed so low that his forehead touched the ground.

"What do I hear? The name of Momotaro? Are you indeed Momotaro? I have often heard of your great strength. Not knowing who you were I have behaved in a very stupid way. Will you please pardon my rudeness? Are you indeed on your way to invade the Island of Devils? If you will take such a rude fellow with you as one of your followers, I shall be very grateful to you."

"I think I can take you with me if you wish to go," said Momotaro.

"Thank you!" said the dog. "By the way, I am very very hungry. Will you give me one of the cakes you are carrying?"

"This is the best kind of cake there is in Japan," said Momotaro. "I cannot spare you a whole one; I will give you half of one."

"Thank you very much," said the dog, taking the piece thrown to him.

Then Momotaro got up and the dog followed. For a long time they walked over the hills and through the valleys. As they were going along an animal came down from a tree a little ahead of them. The creature soon came up to Momotaro and said:

"Good morning, Momotaro! You are welcome in this part of the country. Will you allow me to go with you?"

The dog answered jealously:

"Momotaro already has a dog to accompany him. Of what use is a monkey like you in battle? We are on our way to fight the devils! Get away!"

The dog and the monkey began to quarrel and bite, for these two animals always hate each other.

"Now, don't quarrel!" said Momotaro, putting himself between them. "Wait a moment, dog!"

"It is not at all dignified for you to have such a creature as that following you!" said the dog.

"What do you know about it?" asked Momotaro; and pushing aside the dog, he spoke to the monkey:

"Who are you?"

"I am a monkey living in these hills," replied the monkey. "I heard of your expedition to the Island of Devils, and I have come to go with you. Nothing will please me more than to follow you!"

"Do you really wish to go to the Island of Devils and fight with me?"

"Yes, sir," replied the monkey.

"I admire your courage," said Momotaro. "Here is a piece of one of my fine rice-cakes. Come along!"

So the monkey joined Momotaro. The dog and the monkey did not get on well together. They were always snapping at each other as they went along, and always wanting to have a fight. This made Momotaro very cross, and at last he sent the dog on ahead with a flag and put the monkey behind with a sword, and he placed himself between them with a war-fan, which is made of iron.

By and by they came to a large field. Here a bird flew down and alighted on the ground just in front of the little party. It was the most beautiful bird Momotaro had ever seen. On its body were five different robes of feathers and its head was covered with a scarlet cap.

The dog at once ran at the bird and tried to seize and kill it. But the bird struck out its spurs and flew at the dog's tail, and the fight went hard with both.

Momotaro, as he looked on, could not help admiring the bird; it showed so much spirit in the fight. It would certainly make a good fighter.

Momotaro went up to the two combatants, and holding the dog back, said to the bird:

"You rascal! you are hindering my journey. Surrender at once, and I will take you with me. If you don't I will set this dog to bite your head off!"

Then the bird surrendered at once, and begged to be taken into Momotaro's company.

"I do not know what excuse to offer for quarreling with the dog, your servant, but I did not see you. I am a miserable bird called a pheasant. It is very generous of you to pardon my rudeness and to take me with you. Please allow me to follow you behind the dog and the monkey!"

"I congratulate you on surrendering so soon," said Momotaro, smiling. "Come and join us in our raid on the devils."

"Are you going to take this bird with you also?" asked the dog, interrupting.

"Why do you ask such an unnecessary question? Didn't you hear what I said? I take the bird with me because I wish to!"

"Humph!" said the dog.

Then Momotaro stood and gave this order:

"Now all of you must listen to me. The first thing necessary in an army is harmony. It is a wise saying which says that 'Advantage on earth is better than advantage in Heaven!' Union amongst ourselves is better than any earthly gain. When we are not at peace amongst ourselves it is no easy thing to subdue an enemy. From now, you three, the dog, the monkey and the pheasant, must be friends with one mind. The one who first begins a quarrel will be discharged on the spot!"

All the three promised not to quarrel. The pheasant was now made a member of Momotaro's suite, and received half a cake.

Momotaro's influence was so great that the three became good friends, and hurried onwards with him as their leader.

Hurrying on day after day they at last came out upon the shore of the North-Eastern Sea. There was nothing to be seen as far as the horizon—not a sign of any island. All that broke the stillness was the rolling of the waves upon the shore.

Now, the dog and the monkey and the pheasant had come very bravely all the way through the long valleys and over the hills, but they had never seen the sea before, and for the first time since they set out they were bewildered and gazed at each other in silence. How were they to cross the water and get to the Island of Devils?

Momotaro soon saw that they were daunted by the sight of the sea, and to try them he spoke loudly and roughly:

"Why do you hesitate? Are you afraid of the sea? Oh! what cowards you are! It is impossible to take such weak creatures as you with me to fight the demons. It will be far better for me to go alone. I discharge you all at once!"

The three animals were taken aback at this sharp reproof, and clung to Momotaro's sleeve, begging him not to send them away.

"Please, Momotaro!" said the dog.

"We have come thus far!" said the monkey.

"It is inhuman to leave us here!" said the pheasant.

"We are not at all afraid of the sea," said the monkey again.

"Please do take us with you," said the pheasant.

"Do please," said the dog.

They had now gained a little courage, so Momotaro said:

"Well, then, I will take you with me, but be careful!"

Momotaro now got a small ship, and they all got on board. The wind and weather were fair, and the ship went like an arrow over the sea. It was the first time they had ever been on the water, and so at first the dog, the monkey and the pheasant were frightened at the waves and the rolling of the vessel, but by degrees they grew accustomed to the water and were quite happy again. Every day they paced the deck of their little ship, eagerly looking out for the demons' island.

When they grew tired of this, they told each other stories of all their exploits of which they were proud, and then played games together; and Momotaro found much to amuse him in listening to the three animals and watching their antics, and in this way he forgot that the way was long and that he was tired of the voyage and of doing nothing. He longed to be at work killing the monsters who had done so much harm in his country.

As the wind blew in their favor and they met no storms the ship made a quick voyage, and one day when the sun was shining brightly a sight of land rewarded the four watchers at the bow.

Momotaro knew at once that what they saw was the devils' stronghold. On the top of the precipitous shore, looking out to sea, was a large castle. Now that his enterprise was close at hand, he was deep in thought with his head leaning on his hands, wondering how he should begin the attack. His three followers watched him, waiting for orders. At last he called to the pheasant:

"It is a great advantage for us to have you with us." said Momotaro to the bird, "for you have good wings. Fly at once to the castle and engage the demons to fight. We will follow you."

The pheasant at once obeyed. He flew off from the ship beating the air gladly with his wings. The bird soon reached the island and took up his position on the roof in the middle of the castle, calling out loudly:

"All you devils listen to me! The great Japanese general Momotaro has come to fight you and to take your stronghold from you. If you wish to save your lives surrender at once, and in token of your submission you must break off the horns that grow on your forehead. If you do not surrender at once, but make up your mind to fight, we, the pheasant, the dog and the monkey, will kill you all by biting and tearing you to death!"

The horned demons looking up and only seeing a pheasant, laughed and said:

"A wild pheasant, indeed! It is ridiculous to hear such words from a mean thing like you. Wait till you get a blow from one of our iron bars!"

Very angry, indeed, were the devils. They shook their horns and their shocks of red hair fiercely, and rushed to put on tiger skin trousers to make themselves look more terrible. They then brought out great iron bars and ran to where the pheasant perched over their heads, and tried to knock him down. The pheasant flew to one side to escape the blow, and then attacked the head of first one and then another demon. He flew round and round them, beating the air with his wings so fiercely and ceaselessly, that the devils began to wonder whether they had to fight one or many more birds.

In the meantime, Momotaro had brought his ship to land. As they had approached, he saw that the shore was like a precipice, and that the large castle was surrounded by high walls and large iron gates and was strongly fortified.

Momotaro landed, and with the hope of finding some way of entrance, walked up the path towards the top, followed by the monkey and the dog. They soon came upon two beautiful damsels washing clothes in a stream. Momotaro saw that the clothes were blood-stained, and that as the two maidens washed, the tears were falling fast down their cheeks. He stopped and spoke to them:

"Who are you, and why do you weep?"

"We are captives of the Demon King. We were carried away from our homes to this island, and though we are the daughters of Daimios (Lords), we are obliged to be his servants, and one day he will kill us"—and the maidens held up the blood-stained clothes—"and eat us, and there is no one to help us!"

And their tears burst out afresh at this horrible thought.

"I will rescue you," said Momotaro. "Do not weep any more, only show me how I may get into the castle."

Then the two ladies led the way and showed Momotaro a little back door in the lowest part of the castle wall—so small that Momotaro could hardly crawl in.

The pheasant, who was all this time fighting hard, saw Momotaro and his little band rush in at the back.

Momotaro's onslaught was so furious that the devils could not stand against him. At first their foe had been a single bird, the pheasant, but now that Momotaro and the dog and the monkey had arrived they were bewildered, for the four enemies fought like a hundred, so strong were they. Some of the devils fell off the parapet of the castle and were dashed to pieces on the rocks beneath; others fell into the sea and were drowned; many were beaten to death by the three animals.

The chief of the devils at last was the only one left. He made up his mind to surrender, for he knew that his enemy was stronger than mortal man.

He came up humbly to Momotaro and threw down his iron bar, and kneeling down at the victor's feet he broke off the horns on his head in token of submission, for they were the sign of his strength and power.

"I am afraid of you," he said meekly. "I cannot stand against you. I will give you all the treasure hidden in this castle if you will spare my life!"

Momotaro laughed.

"It is not like you, big devil, to beg for mercy, is it? I cannot spare your wicked life, however much you beg, for you have killed and tortured many people and robbed our country for many years."

Then Momotaro tied the devil chief up and gave him into the monkey's charge. Having done this, he went into all the rooms of the castle and set the prisoners free and gathered together all the treasure he found.

The dog and the pheasant carried home the plunder, and thus Momotaro returned triumphantly to his home, taking with him the devil chief as a captive.

The two poor damsels, daughters of Daimios, and others whom the wicked demon had carried off to be his slaves, were taken safely to their own homes and delivered to their parents.

The whole country made a hero of Momotaro on his triumphant return, and rejoiced that the country was now freed from the robber devils who had been a terror of the land for a long time.

The old couple's joy was greater than ever, and the treasure Momotaro had brought home with him enabled them to live in peace and plenty to the end of their days.

THE HAPPY HUNTER
and the SKILLFUL FISHER

Long, long ago Japan was governed by Hohodemi, the fourth Mikoto (or Augustness) in descent from the illustrious Amaterasu, the Sun Goddess. He was not only as handsome as his ancestress was beautiful, but he was also very strong and brave, and was famous for being the greatest hunter in the land. Because of his matchless skill as a hunter, he was called "Yama-sachi-hiko" or "The Happy Hunter of the Mountains."

His elder brother was a very skillful fisher, and as he far surpassed all rivals in fishing, he was named "Umi-sachi-hiko" or the "Skillful Fisher of the Sea." The brothers thus led happy lives, thoroughly enjoying their respective occupations, and the days passed quickly and pleasantly while each pursued his own way, the one hunting and the other fishing.

One day the Happy Hunter came to his brother, the Skillful Fisher, and said:

"Well, my brother, I see you go to the sea every day with your fishing rod in your hand, and when you return you come laden with fish. And as for me, it is my pleasure to take my bow and arrow and to hunt the wild animals up the mountains and down in the valleys. For a long time we have each followed our favorite occupation, so that now we must both be tired, you of your fishing and I of my hunting. Would it not be wise for us to make a change? Will you try hunting in the mountains and I will go and fish in the sea?"

The Skillful Fisher listened in silence to his brother, and for a moment was thoughtful, but at last he answered:

"O yes, why not? Your idea is not a bad one at all. Give me your bow and arrow and I will set out at once for the mountains and hunt for game."

So the matter was settled by this talk, and the two brothers each started out to try the other's occupation, little dreaming of all that would happen. It was very unwise of them, for the Happy Hunter knew nothing of fishing, and the Skillful Fisher, who was bad tempered, knew as much about hunting.

The Happy Hunter took his brother's much-prized fishing hook and rod and went down to the seashore and sat down on the rocks. He baited his hook and then threw it into the sea clumsily. He sat and gazed at the little float bobbing up and down in the water, and longed for a good fish to come and be caught. Every time the buoy moved a little he pulled up his rod, but there was never a fish at the end of it, only the hook and the bait. If he had known how to fish properly, he would have been able to catch plenty of fish, but although he was the greatest hunter in the land he could not help being the most bungling fisher.

The whole day passed in this way, while he sat on the rocks holding the fishing rod and waiting in vain for his luck to turn. At last the day began to darken, and the evening came; still he had caught not a single fish. Drawing up his line for the last time before going home, he found that he had lost his hook without even knowing when he had dropped it.

He now began to feel extremely anxious, for he knew that his brother would be angry at his having lost his hook, for, it being his only one, he valued it above all other things. The Happy Hunter now set to work to look among the rocks and on the sand for the lost hook, and while he was searching to and fro, his brother, the Skillful Fisher, arrived on the scene. He had failed to find any game while hunting that day, and was not only in a bad temper, but looked fearfully cross. When he saw the Happy Hunter searching about on the shore he knew that something must have gone wrong, so he said at once:

"What are you doing, my brother?"

The Happy Hunter went forward timidly, for he feared his brother's anger, and said:

"Oh, my brother, I have indeed done badly."

"What is the matter?—what have you done?" asked the elder brother impatiently.

"I have lost your precious fishing hook—"

While he was still speaking his brother stopped him, and cried out fiercely:

"Lost my hook! It is just what I expected. For this reason, when you first proposed your plan of changing over our occupations I was really against it, but you seemed to wish it so much that I gave in and allowed you to do as you wished. The mistake of our trying unfamiliar tasks is soon seen! And you have done badly. I will not return you your bow and arrow till you have found my hook. Look to it that you find it and return it to me quickly."

The Happy Hunter felt that he was to blame for all that had come to pass, and bore his brother's scornful scolding with humility and patience. He hunted everywhere for the hook most diligently, but it was nowhere to be found. He was at last obliged to give up all hope of finding it. He then went home, and in desperation broke his beloved sword into pieces and made five hundred hooks out of it.

He took these to his angry brother and offered them to him, asking his forgiveness, and begging him to accept them in the place of the one he had lost for him. It was useless; his brother would not listen to him, much less grant his request.

The Happy Hunter then made another five hundred hooks, and again took them to his brother, beseeching him to pardon him.

"Though you make a million hooks," said the Skillful Fisher, shaking his head, "they are of no use to me. I cannot forgive you unless you bring me back my own hook."

Nothing would appease the anger of the Skillful Fisher, for he had a bad disposition, and had always hated his brother because of his virtues, and now with the excuse of the lost fishing hook he planned to kill him and to usurp his place as ruler of Japan. The Happy Hunter knew all this full well, but he could say nothing, for being the younger he owed his elder brother obedience; so he returned to the seashore and once more began to look for the missing hook. He was much cast down, for he had lost all hope of ever finding his brother's hook now. While he stood on the beach, lost in perplexity and wondering what he had best do next, an old man suddenly appeared carrying a stick in his hand. The Happy Hunter afterwards remembered that he did not see from whence the old man came, neither did he know how he was there—he happened to look up and saw the old man coming towards him.

"You are Hohodemi, the Augustness, sometimes called the Happy Hunter, are you not?" asked the old man. "What are you doing alone in such a place?"

"Yes, I am he," answered the unhappy young man. "Unfortunately, while fishing I lost my brother's precious fishing hook. I have hunted this shore all over, but alas! I cannot find it, and I am very troubled, for my brother won't forgive me till I restore it to him. But who are you?"

"My name is Shiwozuchino Okina, and I live nearby on this shore. I am sorry to hear what misfortune has befallen you. You must indeed be anxious. But if I tell you what I think, the hook is nowhere here—it is either at the bottom of the sea or in the body of some fish who has swallowed it, and for this reason, though you spend your whole life in looking for it here, you will never find it."

"Then what can I do?" asked the distressed man.

"You had better go down to Ryn Gu and tell Ryn Jin, the Dragon King of the Sea, what your trouble is and ask him to find the hook for you. I think that would be the best way."

"Your idea is a splendid one," said the Happy Hunter, "but I fear I cannot get to the Sea King's realm, for I have always heard that it is situated at the bottom of the sea."

"Oh, there will be no difficulty about your getting there," said the old man; "I can soon make something for you to ride on through the sea."

"Thank you," said the Happy Hunter, "I shall be very grateful to you if you will be so kind."

The old man at once set to work, and soon made a basket and offered it to the Happy Hunter. He received it with joy, and taking it to the water, mounted it, and prepared to start. He bade good-by to the kind old man who had helped him so much, and told him that he would certainly reward him as soon as he found his hook and could return to Japan without fear of his brother's anger. The old man pointed out the direction he must take, and told him how to reach the realm of Ryn Gu, and watched him ride out to sea on the basket, which resembled a small boat.

The Happy Hunter made all the haste he could, riding on the basket which had been given him by his friend. His queer boat seemed to go through the water of its own accord, and the distance was much shorter than he had expected, for in a few hours he caught sight of the gate and the roof of the Sea King's Palace. And what a large place it was, with its numberless sloping roofs and gables, its huge gateways, and its gray stone walls! He soon landed, and leaving his basket on the beach, he walked up to the large gateway. The pillars of the gate were made of beautiful red coral, and the gate itself was adorned with glittering gems of all kinds. Large *katsura* trees overshadowed it. Our hero had often heard of the wonders of the Sea King's Palace beneath the sea, but all the stories he had ever heard fell short of the reality which he now saw for the first time.

The Happy Hunter would have liked to enter the gate there and then, but he saw that it was fast closed, and also that there was no one about whom he could ask to open it for him, so he stopped to think what he should do. In the shade of the trees before the gate he noticed a well full of fresh spring water. Surely some one would come out to draw water from the well some time, he thought. Then he climbed into the tree overhanging the well, and seated himself to rest on one of the branches, and waited for what might happen. Ere long he saw the huge gate swing open, and two beautiful women came out. Now the Mikoto (Augustness) had always heard that Ryn Gu was the realm of the Dragon King under the Sea, and had naturally supposed that the place was inhabited by dragons and similar terrible creatures, so that when he saw these two lovely princesses, whose beauty would be rare even in the world from which he had just come, he was exceedingly surprised, and wondered what it could mean.

He said not a word, however, but silently gazed at them through the foliage of the trees, waiting to see what they would do. He saw that in their hands they carried golden buckets. Slowly and gracefully in their trailing garments they approached the well, standing in the shade of the *katsura* trees, and were about to draw water, all unknowing of the stranger who was watching them, for the Happy Hunter was quite hidden among the branches of the tree where he had posted himself.

As the two ladies leaned over the side of the well to let down their golden buckets, which they did every day in the year, they saw reflected in the deep still water the face of a handsome youth gazing at them from amidst the branches of the tree in whose shade they stood. Never before had they seen the face of mortal man; they were frightened, and drew back quickly with their golden buckets in their hands. Their curiosity, however, soon gave them courage, and they glanced timidly upwards to see the cause of the unusual reflection, and then they beheld the Happy Hunter sitting in the tree looking down at them with surprise and admiration. They gazed at him face to face, but their tongues were still with wonder and could not find a word to say to him.

When the Mikoto saw that he was discovered, he sprang down lightly from the tree and said:

"I am a traveler, and as I was very thirsty I came to the well in the hopes of quenching my thirst, but I could find no bucket with which to draw the water.

So I climbed into the tree, much vexed, and waited for some one to come. Just at that moment, while I was thirstily and impatiently waiting, you noble ladies appeared, as if in answer to my great need. Therefore I pray you of your mercy give me some water to drink, for I am a thirsty traveler in a strange land."

His dignity and graciousness overruled their timidity, and bowing in silence they both once more approached the well, and letting down their golden buckets drew up some water and poured it into a jeweled cup and offered it to the stranger.

He received it from them with both hands, raising it to the height of his forehead in token of high respect and pleasure, and then drank the water quickly, for his thirst was great. When he had finished his long draught he set the cup down on the edge of the well, and drawing his short sword he cut off one of the strange curved jewels (*magatama*), a necklace of which hung round his neck and fell over his breast. He placed the jewel in the cup and returned it to them, and said, bowing deeply:

"This is a token of my thanks!"

The two ladies took the cup, and looking into it to see what he had put inside—for they did not yet know what it was—they gave a start of surprise, for there lay a beautiful gem at the bottom of the cup.

"No ordinary mortal would give away a jewel so freely. Will you not honor us by telling us who you are?" said the elder damsel.

"Certainly," said the Happy Hunter. "I am Hohodemi, the fourth Mikoto, also called in Japan, the Happy Hunter."

"Are you indeed Hohodemi, the grandson of Amaterasu, the Sun Goddess?" asked the damsel who had spoken first. "I am the eldest daughter of Ryn Jin, the King of the Sea, and my name is Princess Tayotama."

"And," said the younger maiden, who at last found her tongue, "I am her sister, the Princess Tamayori."

"Are you indeed the daughters of Ryn Jin, the King of the Sea? I cannot tell you how glad I am to meet you," said the Happy Hunter. And without waiting for them to reply he went on:

"The other day I went fishing with my brother's hook and dropped it, how, I am sure I can't tell. As my brother prizes his fishing hook above all his other possessions, this is the greatest calamity that could have befallen me. Unless I find it again I can never hope to win my brother's forgiveness, for he is very angry at what I have done. I have searched for it many, many times, but I cannot find it, therefore I am much troubled. While I was hunting for the hook, in great distress, I met a wise old man, and he told me that the best thing I could do was to come to Ryn Gu, and to Ryn Jin, the Dragon King of the Sea, and ask him to help me. This kind old man also showed me how to come. Now you know how it is I am here and why. I want to ask Ryn Jin if he knows where the lost hook is. Will you be so kind as to take me to your father? And do you think he will see me?" asked the Happy Hunter anxiously.

Princess Tayotama listened to this long story, and then said:

"Not only is it easy for you to see my father, but he will be much pleased to meet you. I am sure he will say that good fortune has befallen him, that so great and noble a man as you, the grandson of Amaterasu, should come down to the bottom of the sea." And then turning to her younger sister, she said:

"Do you not think so, Tamayori?"

"Yes, indeed," answered the Princess Tamayori, in her sweet voice. "As you say, we can know no greater honor than to welcome the Mikoto to our home."

"Then I ask you to be so kind as to lead the way," said the Happy Hunter.

"Condescend to enter, Mikoto (Augustness)," said both the sisters, and bowing low, they led him through the gate.

The younger Princess left her sister to take charge of the Happy Hunter, and going faster than they, she reached the Sea King's Palace first, and running quickly to her father's room, she told him of all that had happened to them at the gate, and that her sister was even now bringing the Augustness to him. The Dragon King of the Sea was much surprised at the news, for it was but seldom, perhaps only once in several hundred years, that the Sea King's Palace was visited by mortals.

Ryn Jin at once clapped his hands and summoned all his courtiers and the servants of the Palace, and the chief fish of the sea together, and solemnly told them that the grandson of the Sun Goddess, Amaterasu, was coming to the Palace, and that they must be very ceremonious and polite in serving the august visitor. He then ordered them all to the entrance of the Palace to welcome the Happy Hunter.

Ryn Jin then dressed himself in his robes of ceremony, and went out to welcome him. In a few moments the Princess Tayotama and the Happy Hunter reached the entrance, and the Sea King and his wife bowed to the ground and thanked him for the honor he did them in coming to see them. The Sea King then led the Happy Hunter to the guest room, and placing him in the uppermost seat, he bowed respectfully before him, and said:

"I am Ryn Jin, the Dragon King of the Sea, and this is my wife. Condescend to remember us forever!"

"Are you indeed Ryn Jin, the King of the Sea, of whom I have so often heard?" answered the Happy Hunter, saluting his host most ceremoniously. "I must apologize for all the trouble I am giving you by my unexpected visit." And he bowed again, and thanked the Sea King.

"You need not thank me," said Ryn Jin. "It is I who must thank you for coming. Although the Sea Palace is a poor place, as you see, I shall be highly honored if you will make us a long visit."

There was much gladness between the Sea King and the Happy Hunter, and they sat and talked for a long time. At last the Sea King clapped his hands, and then a huge retinue of fishes appeared, all robed in ceremonial garments, and bearing in their fins various trays on which all kinds of sea delicacies were served. A great feast was now spread before the King and his Royal guest. All the fishes-in-waiting were chosen from amongst the finest fish in the sea, so you can imagine what a wonderful array of sea creatures it was that waited upon the Happy Hunter that day. All in the Palace tried to do their best to please him and to show him that he was a much honored guest. During the long repast, which lasted for hours, Ryn Jin commanded his daughters to play some music, and the two Princesses came in and performed on the *koto* (the Japanese harp), and sang and danced in turns. The time passed so pleasantly that the Happy Hunter seemed to forget his trouble and why he had come at all to the Sea King's Realm, and he gave himself up to the enjoyment of this wonderful place, the land of fairy fishes! Who has ever heard of such a marvelous place? But the Mikoto soon remembered what had brought him to Ryn Gu, and said to his host:

"Perhaps your daughters have told you, King Ryn Jin, that I have come here to try and recover my brother's fishing hook, which I lost while fishing the other day. May I ask you to be so kind as to inquire of all your subjects if any of them have seen a fishing hook lost in the sea?"

"Certainly," said the obliging Sea King, "I will immediately summon them all here and ask them."

As soon as he had issued his command, the octopus, the cuttlefish, the bonito, the oxtail fish, the eel, the jelly fish, the shrimp, and the plaice, and many other fishes of all kinds came in and sat down before Ryn Jin their King, and arranged themselves and their fins in order. Then the Sea King said solemnly:

"Our visitor who is sitting before you all is the august grandson of Amaterasu. His name is Hohodemi, the fourth Augustness, and he is also called the Happy Hunter of the Mountains. While he was fishing the other day upon the shore of Japan, some one robbed him of his brother's fishing hook. He has come all this way down to the bottom of the sea to our Kingdom because he thought that one of you fishes may have taken the hook from him in mischievous play. If any of you have done so you must immediately return it, or if any of you know who the thief is you must at once tell us his name and where he is now."

All the fishes were taken by surprise when they heard these words, and could say nothing for some time. They sat looking at each other and at the Dragon King. At last the cuttlefish came forward and said:

"I think the *tai* (the red bream) must be the thief who has stolen the hook!"

"Where is your proof?" asked the King.

"Since yesterday evening the *tai* has not been able to eat anything, and he seems to be suffering from a bad throat! For this reason I think the hook may be in his throat. You had better send for him at once!"

All the fish agreed to this, and said:

"It is certainly strange that the *tai* is the only fish who has not obeyed your summons. Will you send for him and inquire into the matter. Then our innocence will be proved."

"Yes," said the Sea King, "it is strange that the *tai* has not come, for he ought to be the first to be here. Send for him at once!"

Without waiting for the King's order the cuttlefish had already started for the *tai*'s dwelling, and he now returned, bringing the *tai* with him. He led him before the King.

The *tai* sat there looking frightened and ill. He certainly was in pain, for his usually red face was pale, and his eyes were nearly closed and looked but half their usual size.

"Answer, O *Tai*!" cried the Sea King, "why did you not come in answer to my summons today?"

"I have been ill since yesterday," answered the *tai*; "that is why I could not come."

"Don't say another word!" cried out Ryn Jin angrily. "Your illness is the punishment of the gods for stealing the Mikoto's hook."

"It is only too true!" said the *tai*; "the hook is still in my throat, and all my efforts to get it out have been useless. I can't eat, and I can scarcely breathe, and each moment I feel that it will choke me, and sometimes it gives me great pain. I had no intention of stealing the Mikoto's hook. I heedlessly snapped at the bait which I saw in the water, and the hook came off and stuck in my throat. So I hope you will pardon me."

The cuttlefish now came forward, and said to the King:

"What I said was right. You see the hook still sticks in the *tai*'s throat. I hope to be able to pull it out in the presence of the Mikoto, and then we can return it to him safely!"

"O please make haste and pull it out!" cried the *tai*, pitifully, for he felt the pains in his throat coming on again; "I do so want to return the hook to the Mikoto."

"All right, *Tai San*," said his friend the cuttlefish, and then opening the *tai*'s mouth as wide as he could and putting one of his feelers down the *tai*'s throat, he quickly and easily drew the hook out of the sufferer's large mouth. He then washed it and brought it to the King.

Ryn Jin took the hook from his subject, and then respectfully returned it to the Happy Hunter (the Mikoto or Augustness, the fishes called him), who was overjoyed at getting back his hook. He thanked Ryn Jin many times, his face beaming with gratitude, and said that he owed the happy ending of his quest to the Sea King's wise authority and kindness.

Ryn Jin now desired to punish the *tai*, but the Happy Hunter begged him not to do so; since his lost hook was thus happily recovered he did not wish to make more trouble for the poor *tai*. It was indeed the *tai* who had taken the hook, but he had already suffered enough for his fault, if fault it could be called. What had been done was done in heedlessness and not by intention. The Happy Hunter said he blamed himself; if he had understood how to fish properly he would never have lost his hook, and therefore all this trouble had been caused in the first place by his trying to do something which he did not know how to do. So he begged the Sea King to forgive his subject.

Who could resist the pleading of so wise and compassionate a judge? Ryn Jin forgave his subject at once at the request of his august guest. The *tai* was so glad that he shook his fins for joy, and he and all the other fish went out from the presence of their King, praising the virtues of the Happy Hunter.

Now that the hook was found the Happy Hunter had nothing to keep him in Ryn Gu, and he was anxious to get back to his own kingdom and to make peace with his angry brother, the Skillful Fisher; but the Sea King, who had learnt to love him and would fain have kept him as a son, begged him not to go so soon, but to make the Sea Palace his home as long as ever he liked. While the Happy Hunter was still hesitating, the two lovely Princesses, Tayotama and Tamayori, came, and with the sweetest of bows and voices joined with their father in pressing him to stay, so that without seeming ungracious he could not say them "Nay," and was obliged to stay on for some time.

Between the Sea Realm and the Earth there was no difference in the night of time, and the Happy Hunter found that three years went fleeting quickly by in this delightful land. The years pass swiftly when any one is truly happy. But though the wonders of that enchanted land seemed to be new every day, and though the Sea King's kindness seemed rather to increase than to grow less with time, the Happy Hunter grew more and more homesick as the days passed, and he could not repress a great anxiety to know what had happened to his home and his country and his brother while he had been away.

So at last he went to the Sea King and said:

"My stay with you here has been most happy and I am very grateful to you for all your kindness to me, but I govern Japan, and, delightful as this place is, I cannot absent myself forever from my country. I must also return the fishing hook to my brother and ask his forgiveness for having deprived him of it for so long. I am indeed very sorry to part from you, but this time it cannot be helped. With your gracious permission, I will take my leave to-day. I hope to make you another visit some day. Please give up the idea of my staying longer now."

King Ryn Jin was overcome with sorrow at the thought that he must lose his friend who had made a great diversion in the Palace of the Sea, and his tears fell fast as he answered:

"We are indeed very sorry to part with you, Mikoto, for we have enjoyed your stay with us very much. You have been a noble and honored guest and we have heartily made you welcome. I quite understand that as you govern Japan you ought to be there and not here, and that it is vain for us to try and keep you longer with us, much as we would like to have you stay. I hope you will not forget us. Strange circumstances have brought us together and I trust the friendship thus begun between the Land and the Sea will last and grow stronger than it has ever been before."

When the Sea King had finished speaking he turned to his two daughters and bade them bring him the two Tide-Jewels of the Sea. The two Princesses bowed low, rose and glided out of the hall. In a few minutes they returned, each one carrying in her hands a flashing gem which filled the room with light. As the Happy Hunter looked at them he wondered what they could be. The Sea King took them from his daughters and said to his guest:

"These two valuable talismans we have inherited from our ancestors from time immemorial. We now give them to you as a parting gift in token of our great affection for you. These two gems are called the *Nanjiu* and the *Kanjiu*."

The Happy Hunter bowed low to the ground and said:

"I can never thank you enough for all your kindness to me. And now will you add one more favor to the rest and tell me what these jewels are and what I am to do with them?"

"The *Nanjiu*," answered the Sea King, "is also called the Jewel of the Flood Tide, and whoever holds it in his possession can command the sea to roll in and to flood the land at any time that he wills. The *Kanjiu* is also called the Jewel of the Ebbing Tide, and this gem controls the sea and the waves thereof, and will cause even a tidal wave to recede."

Then Ryn Jin showed his friend how to use the talismans one by one and handed them to him. The Happy Hunter was very glad to have these two wonderful gems, the Jewel of the Flood Tide and the Jewel of the Ebbing Tide, to take back with him, for he felt that they would preserve him in case of danger from enemies at any time. After thanking his kind host again and again, he prepared to depart. The Sea King and the two Princesses, Tayotama and Tamayori, and all the inmates of the Palace, came out to say "Good-by," and before the sound of the last farewell had died away the Happy Hunter passed out from under the gateway, past the well of happy memory standing in the shade of the great *katsura* trees on his way to the beach.

Here he found, instead of the queer basket on which he had come to the Realm of Ryn Gu, a large crocodile waiting for him. Never had he seen such a huge creature. It measured eight fathoms in length from the tip of its tail to the end of its long mouth. The Sea King had ordered the monster to carry the Happy Hunter back to Japan. Like the wonderful basket which Shiwozuchino Okina had made, it could travel faster than any steamboat, and in this strange way, riding on the back of a crocodile, the Happy Hunter returned to his own land.

As soon as the crocodile landed him, the Happy Hunter hastened to tell the Skillful Fisher of his safe return. He then gave him back the fishing hook which had been found in the mouth of the *tai* and which had been the cause of so much trouble between them. He earnestly begged his brother's forgiveness, telling him all that had happened to him in the Sea King's Palace and what wonderful adventures had led to the finding of the hook.

Now the Skillful Fisher had used the lost hook as an excuse for driving his brother out of the country. When his brother had left him that day three years ago, and had not returned, he had been very glad in his evil heart and had at once usurped his brother's place as ruler of the land, and had become powerful and rich. Now in the midst of enjoying what did not belong to him, and hoping that his brother might never return to claim his rights, quite unexpectedly there stood the Happy Hunter before him.

The Skillful Fisher feigned forgiveness, for he could make no more excuses for sending his brother away again, but in his heart he was very angry and hated his brother more and more, till at last he could no longer bear the sight of him day after day, and planned and watched for an opportunity to kill him.

One day when the Happy Hunter was walking in the rice fields his brother followed him with a dagger. The Happy Hunter knew that his brother was following him to kill him, and he felt that now, in this hour of great danger, was the time to use the Jewels of the Flow and Ebb of the Tide and prove whether what the Sea King had told him was true or not.

So he took out the Jewel of the Flood Tide from the bosom of his dress and raised it to his forehead. Instantly over the fields and over the farms the sea came rolling in wave upon wave till it reached the spot where his brother was standing. The Skillful Fisher stood amazed and terrified to see what was happening. In another minute he was struggling in the water and calling on his brother to save him from drowning.

The Happy Hunter had a kind heart and could not bear the sight of his brother's distress. He at once put back the Jewel of the Flood Tide and took out the Jewel of the Ebb Tide. No sooner did he hold it up as high as his forehead than the sea ran back and back, and ere long the tossing rolling floods had vanished, and the farms and fields and dry land appeared as before.

The Skillful Fisher was very frightened at the peril of death in which he had stood, and was greatly impressed by the wonderful things he had seen his brother do. He learned now that he was making a fatal mistake to set himself against his brother, younger than he though he was, for he now had become so powerful that the sea would flow in and the tide ebb at his word of command. So he humbled himself before the Happy Hunter and asked him to forgive him all the wrong he had done him. The Skillful Fisher promised to restore his brother to his rights and also swore that though the Happy Hunter was the younger brother and owed him allegiance by right of birth, that he, the Skillful Fisher, would exalt him as his superior and bow before him as Lord of all Japan.

Then the Happy Hunter said that he would forgive his brother if he would throw into the receding tide all his evil ways. The Skillful Fisher promised and there was peace between the two brothers. From this time he kept his word and became a good man and a kind brother.

The Happy Hunter now ruled his Kingdom without being disturbed by family strife, and there was peace in Japan for a long, long time. Above all the treasures in his house he prized the wonderful Jewels of the Flow and Ebb of the Tide which had been given him by Ryn Jin, the Dragon King of the Sea.

This is the congratulatory ending of the Happy Hunter and the Skillful Fisher.

THE BAMBOO-CUTTER
and the MOON-CHILD

L ong, long ago, there lived an old bamboo wood-cutter. He was very
poor and sad also, for no child had Heaven sent to cheer his old age,
and in his heart there was no hope of rest from work till he died and
was laid in the quiet grave. Every morning he went forth into the woods
and hills wherever the bamboo reared its lithe green plumes against the sky.
When he had made his choice, he would cut down these feathers of the forest, and splitting them lengthwise, or cutting them into joints, would carry
the bamboo wood home and make it into various articles for the household,
and he and his old wife gained a small livelihood by selling them.

One morning as usual he had gone out to his work, and having found a
nice clump of bamboos, had set to work to cut some of them down. Suddenly
the green grove of bamboos was flooded with a bright soft light, as if the full
moon had risen over the spot. Looking round in astonishment, he saw that
the brilliance was streaming from one bamboo. The old man, full of wonder,
dropped his ax and went towards the light. On nearer approach he saw that
this soft splendor came from a hollow in the green bamboo stem, and still
more wonderful to behold, in the midst of the brilliance stood a tiny human
being, only three inches in height, and exquisitely beautiful in appearance.

"You must be sent to be my child, for I find you here among the bamboos where lies my daily work," said the old man, and taking the little

creature in his hand he took it home to his wife to bring up. The tiny girl was so exceedingly beautiful and so small, that the old woman put her into a basket to safeguard her from the least possibility of being hurt in any way.

The old couple were now very happy, for it had been a lifelong regret that they had no children of their own, and with joy they now expended all the love of their old age on the little child who had come to them in so marvelous a manner.

From this time on, the old man often found gold in the notches of the bamboos when he hewed them down and cut them up; not only gold, but precious stones also, so that by degrees he became rich. He built himself a fine house, and was no longer known as the poor bamboo woodcutter, but as a wealthy man.

Three months passed quickly away, and in that time the bamboo child had, wonderful to say, become a full-grown girl, so her foster-parents did up her hair and dressed her in beautiful *kimonos*. She was of such wondrous beauty that they placed her behind the screens like a princess, and allowed no one to see her, waiting upon her themselves. It seemed as if she were made of light, for the house was filled with a soft shining, so that even in the dark of night it was like daytime. Her presence seemed to have a benign influence on those there. Whenever the old man felt sad, he had only to look upon his foster-daughter and his sorrow vanished, and he became as happy as when he was a youth.

At last the day came for the naming of their new-found child, so the old couple called in a celebrated name-giver, and he gave her the name of Princess Moonlight, because her body gave forth so much soft bright light that she might have been a daughter of the Moon God.

For three days the festival was kept up with song and dance and music. All the friends and relations of the old couple were present, and great was their enjoyment of the festivities held to celebrate the naming of Princess Moonlight. Everyone who saw her declared that there never had been seen any one so lovely; all the beauties throughout the length and breadth of the land would grow pale beside her, so they said. The fame of the Princess's loveliness spread far and wide, and many were the suitors who desired to win her hand, or even so much as to see her.

Suitors from far and near posted themselves outside the house, and made little holes in the fence, in the hope of catching a glimpse of the Princess as she went from one room to the other along the veranda. They stayed there day and night, sacrificing even their sleep for a chance of seeing her, but all in vain. Then they approached the house, and tried to speak to the old man and his wife or some of the servants, but not even this was granted them.

Still, in spite of all this disappointment they stayed on day after day, and night after night, and counted it as nothing, so great was their desire to see the Princess.

At last, however, most of the men, seeing how hopeless their quest was, lost heart and hope both, and returned to their homes. All except five Knights, whose ardor and determination, instead of waning, seemed to wax greater with obstacles. These five men even went without their meals, and took snatches of whatever they could get brought to them, so that they might always stand outside the dwelling. They stood there in all weathers, in sunshine and in rain.

Sometimes they wrote letters to the Princess, but no answer was vouch-safed to them. Then when letters failed to draw any reply, they wrote poems to her telling her of the hopeless love which kept them from sleep, from food, from rest, and even from their homes. Still Princess Moonlight gave no sign of having received their verses.

In this hopeless state the winter passed. The snow and frost and the cold winds gradually gave place to the gentle warmth of spring. Then the summer came, and the sun burned white and scorching in the heavens above and on the earth beneath, and still these faithful Knights kept watch and waited. At the end of these long months they called out to the old bamboo-cutter and entreated him to have some mercy upon them and to show them the Princess, but he answered only that as he was not her real father he could not insist on her obeying him against her wishes.

The five Knights on receiving this stern answer returned to their several homes, and pondered over the best means of touching the proud Princess's heart, even so much as to grant them a hearing. They took their rosaries in hand and knelt before their household shrines, and burned precious incense, praying to Buddha to give them their heart's desire. Thus several days passed, but even so they could not rest in their homes.

So again they set out for the bamboo-cutter's house. This time the old man came out to see them, and they asked him to let them know if it was the Princess's resolution never to see any man whatsoever, and they implored him to speak for them and to tell her the greatness of their love, and how long they had waited through the cold of winter and the heat of summer, sleepless and roofless through all weathers, without food and without rest, in the ardent hope of winning her, and they were willing to consider this long vigil as pleasure if she would but give them one chance of pleading their cause with her.

The old man lent a willing ear to their tale of love, for in his inmost heart he felt sorry for these faithful suitors and would have liked to see his lovely foster-daughter married to one of them. So he went in to Princess Moonlight and said reverently:

"Although you have always seemed to me to be a heavenly being, yet I have had the trouble of bringing you up as my own child and you have been glad of the protection of my roof. Will you refuse to do as I wish?"

Then Princess Moonlight replied that there was nothing she would not do for him, that she honored and loved him as her own father, and that as for herself she could not remember the time before she came to earth.

The old man listened with great joy as she spoke these dutiful words. Then he told her how anxious he was to see her safely and happily married before he died.

"I am an old man, over seventy years of age, and my end may come any time now. It is necessary and right that you should see these five suitors and choose one of them."

"Oh, why," said the Princess in distress, "must I do this? I have no wish to marry now."

"I found you," answered the old man, "many years ago, when you were a little creature three inches high, in the midst of a great white light. The light streamed from the bamboo in which you were hid and led me to you. So I have always thought that you were more than mortal woman. While I am alive it is right for you to remain as you are if you wish to do so, but some day I shall cease to be and who will take care of you then? Therefore I pray you to meet these five brave men one at a time and make up your mind to marry one of them!"

Then the Princess answered that she felt sure that she was not as beautiful as perhaps report made her out to be, and that even if she consented to marry any one of them, not really knowing her before, his heart might change afterwards. So as she did not feel sure of them, even though her father told her they were worthy Knights, she did not feel it wise to see them.

"All you say is very reasonable," said the old man, "but what kind of men will you consent to see? I do not call these five men who have waited on you for months, light-hearted. They have stood outside this house through the winter and the summer, often denying themselves food and sleep so that they may win you. What more can you demand?"

Then Princess Moonlight said she must make further trial of their love before she would grant their request to interview her. The five warriors were to prove their love by each bringing her from distant countries something that she desired to possess.

That same evening the suitors arrived and began to play their flutes in turn, and to sing their self-composed songs telling of their great and tireless love. The bamboo-cutter went out to them and offered them his sympathy for all they had endured and all the patience they had shown in their desire to win his foster-daughter. Then he gave them her message, that she would consent to marry whosoever was successful in bringing her what she wanted. This was to test them.

The five all accepted the trial, and thought it an excellent plan, for it would prevent jealousy between them.

Princess Moonlight then sent word to the First Knight that she requested him to bring her the stone bowl which had belonged to Buddha in India.

The Second Knight was asked to go to the Mountain of Horai, said to be situated in the Eastern Sea, and to bring her a branch of the wonderful tree that grew on its summit. The roots of this tree were of silver, the trunk of gold, and the branches bore as fruit white jewels.

The Third Knight was told to go to China and search for the fire-rat and to bring her its skin.

The Fourth Knight was told to search for the dragon that carried on its head the stone radiating five colors and to bring the stone to her.

The Fifth Knight was to find the swallow which carried a shell in its stomach and to bring the shell to her.

The old man thought these very hard tasks and hesitated to carry the messages, but the Princess would make no other conditions. So her commands were issued word for word to the five men who, when they heard what was required of them, were all disheartened and disgusted at what seemed to them the impossibility of the tasks given them and returned to their own homes in despair.

But after a time, when they thought of the Princess, the love in their hearts revived for her, and they resolved to make an attempt to get what she desired of them.

The First Knight sent word to the Princess that he was starting out that day on the quest of Buddha's bowl, and he hoped soon to bring it to her. But he had not the courage to go all the way to India, for in those days traveling was very difficult and full of danger, so he went to one of the temples in Kyoto and took a stone bowl from the altar there, paying the priest a large sum of money for it. He then wrapped it in a cloth of gold and, waiting quietly for three years, returned and carried it to the old man.

Princess Moonlight wondered that the Knight should have returned so soon. She took the bowl from its gold wrapping, expecting it to make the room full of light, but it did not shine at all, so she knew that it was a sham thing and not the true bowl of Buddha. She returned it at once and refused to see him. The Knight threw the bowl away and returned to his home in despair. He gave up now all hopes of ever winning the Princess.

The Second Knight told his parents that he needed change of air for his health, for he was ashamed to tell them that love for the Princess Moonlight was the real cause of his leaving them. He then left his home, at the same time sending word to the Princess that he was setting out for Mount Horai in the hope of getting her a branch of the gold and silver tree which she so much wished to have. He only allowed his servants to accompany him half-way, and then sent them back. He reached the seashore and embarked on a small ship, and after sailing away for three days he landed and employed several carpenters to build him a house contrived in such a way that no one could get access to it. He then shut himself up with six skilled jewelers, and endeavored to make such a gold and silver branch as he thought would satisfy the Princess as having come from the wonderful tree growing on Mount Horai. Every one whom he had asked declared that Mount Horai belonged to the land of fable and not to fact.

When the branch was finished, he took his journey home and tried to make himself look as if he were wearied and worn out with travel. He put the jeweled branch into a lacquer box and carried it to the bamboo-cutter, begging him to present it to the Princess.

The old man was quite deceived by the travel-stained appearance of the Knight, and thought that he had only just returned from his long journey with the branch. So he tried to persuade the Princess to consent to see the man. But she remained silent and looked very sad. The old man began to take out the branch and praised it as a wonderful treasure to be found nowhere in the whole land. Then he spoke of the Knight, how handsome and how brave he was to have undertaken a journey to so remote a place as the Mount of Horai.

Princess Moonlight took the branch in her hand and looked at it carefully. She then told her foster-parent that she knew it was impossible for the man to have obtained a branch from the gold and silver tree growing on Mount Horai so quickly or so easily, and she was sorry to say she believed it artificial.

The old man then went out to the expectant Knight, who had now approached the house, and asked where he had found the branch. Then the man did not scruple to make up a long story.

"Two years ago I took a ship and started in search of Mount Horai. After going before the wind for some time I reached the far Eastern Sea. Then a great storm arose and I was tossed about for many days, losing all count of the points of the compass, and finally we were blown ashore on an unknown island. Here I found the place inhabited by demons who at one time threatened to kill and eat me. However, I managed to make friends with these horrible creatures, and they helped me and my sailors to repair the boat, and I set sail again. Our food gave out, and we suffered much from sickness on board. At last, on the five-hundredth day from the day of starting, I saw far off on the horizon what looked like the peak of a mountain. On nearer approach, this proved to be an island, in the center of which rose a high mountain. I landed, and after wandering about for two or three days, I saw a shining being coming towards me on the beach, holding in his hands a golden bowl. I went up to him and asked him if I had, by good chance, found the island of Mount Horai, and he answered: 'Yes, this is Mount Horai!'

"With much difficulty I climbed to the summit, where stood the golden tree growing with silver roots in the ground. The wonders of that strange land are many, and if I began to tell you about them I could never stop. In spite of my wish to stay there long, on breaking off the branch I hurried back. With utmost speed it has taken me four hundred days to get back, and, as you see, my clothes are still damp from exposure on the long sea voyage. I have not even waited to change my raiment, so anxious was I to bring the branch to the Princess quickly."

Just at this moment the six jewelers, who had been employed on the making of the branch, but not yet paid by the Knight, arrived at the house and sent in a petition to the Princess to be paid for their labor. They said that they had worked for over a thousand days making the branch of gold, with its silver twigs and its jeweled fruit, that was now presented to her by the Knight, but as yet they had received nothing in payment. So this Knight's deception was thus found out, and the Princess, glad of an escape from one more importunate suitor, was only too pleased to send back the branch. She called in the workmen and had them paid liberally, and they went away happy. But on the way home they were overtaken by the disappointed man, who beat them till they were nearly dead, for letting out the secret, and they barely escaped with their lives. The Knight then returned home, raging in his heart; and in despair of ever winning the Princess gave up society and retired to a solitary life among the mountains.

Now the Third Knight had a friend in China, so he wrote to him to get the skin of the fire-rat. The virtue of any part of this animal was that no fire could harm it. He promised his friend any amount of money he liked to ask if only he could get him the desired article. As soon as the news came that the ship on which his friend had sailed home had come into port, he rode seven days on horseback to meet him. He handed his friend a large sum of money, and received the fire-rat's skin. When he reached home he put it carefully in a box and sent it in to the Princess while he waited outside for her answer.

The bamboo-cutter took the box from the Knight and, as usual, carried it in to her and tried to coax her to see the Knight at once, but Princess

Moonlight refused, saying that she must first put the skin to test by putting it into the fire. If it were the real thing it would not burn. So she took off the crape wrapper and opened the box, and then threw the skin into the fire. The skin crackled and burnt up at once, and the Princess knew that this man also had not fulfilled his word. So the Third Knight failed also.

Now the Fourth Knight was no more enterprising than the rest. Instead of starting out on the quest of the dragon bearing on its head the five-color-radiating jewel, he called all his servants together and gave them the order to seek for it far and wide in Japan and in China, and he strictly forbade any of them to return till they had found it.

His numerous retainers and servants started out in different directions, with no intention, however, of obeying what they considered an impossible order. They simply took a holiday, went to pleasant country places together, and grumbled at their master's unreasonableness.

The Knight meanwhile, thinking that his retainers could not fail to find the jewel, repaired to his house, and fitted it up beautifully for the reception of the Princess, he felt so sure of winning her.

One year passed away in weary waiting, and still his men did not return with the dragon-jewel. The Knight became desperate. He could wait no longer, so taking with him only two men he hired a ship and commanded the captain to go in search of the dragon; the captain and the sailors refused to undertake what they said was an absurd search, but the Knight compelled them at last to put out to sea.

When they had been but a few days out they encountered a great storm which lasted so long that, by the time its fury abated, the Knight had determined to give up the hunt of the dragon. They were at last blown on shore, for navigation was primitive in those days. Worn out with his travels and anxiety, the fourth suitor gave himself up to rest. He had caught a very heavy cold, and had to go to bed with a swollen face.

The governor of the place, hearing of his plight, sent messengers with a letter inviting him to his house. While he was there thinking over all his troubles, his love for the Princess turned to anger, and he blamed her for all the hardships he had undergone. He thought that it was quite probable she had wished to kill him so that she might be rid of him, and in order to carry out her wish had sent him upon his impossible quest.

At this point all the servants he had sent out to find the jewel came to see him, and were surprised to find praise instead of displeasure awaiting them. Their master told them that he was heartily sick of adventure, and said that he never intended to go near the Princess's house again in the future.

Like all the rest, the Fifth Knight failed in his quest—he could not find the swallow's shell.

By this time the fame of Princess Moonlight's beauty had reached the ears of the Emperor, and he sent one of the Court ladies to see if she were really as lovely as report said; if so he would summon her to the Palace and make her one of the ladies-in-waiting.

When the Court lady arrived, in spite of her father's entreaties, Princess Moonlight refused to see her. The Imperial messenger insisted, saying it was the Emperor's order. Then Princess Moonlight told the old man that if she was forced to go to the Palace in obedience to the Emperor's order, she would vanish from the earth.

When the Emperor was told of her persistence in refusing to obey his summons, and that if pressed to obey she would disappear altogether from sight, he determined to go and see her. So he planned to go on a hunting excursion in the neighborhood of the bamboo-cutter's house, and see the Princess himself. He sent word to the old man of his intention, and he received consent to the scheme. The next day the Emperor set out with his retinue, which he soon managed to outride. He found the bamboo-cutter's house and dismounted. He then entered the house and went straight to where the Princess was sitting with her attendant maidens.

Never had he seen any one so wonderfully beautiful, and he could not but look at her, for she was more lovely than any human being as she shone in her own soft radiance. When Princess Moonlight became aware that a stranger was looking at her she tried to escape from the room, but the Emperor caught her and begged her to listen to what he had to say. Her only answer was to hide her face in her sleeves.

The Emperor fell deeply in love with her, and begged her to come to the Court, where he would give her a position of honor and everything she could wish for. He was about to send for one of the Imperial palanquins to take her back with him at once, saying that her grace and beauty should adorn a Court, and not be hidden in a bamboo-cutter's cottage.

But the Princess stopped him. She said that if she were forced to go to the Palace she would turn at once into a shadow, and even as she spoke she began to lose her form. Her figure faded from his sight while he looked.

The Emperor then promised to leave her free if only she would resume her former shape, which she did.

It was now time for him to return, for his retinue would be wondering what had happened to their Royal master when they missed him for so long. So he bade her good-by, and left the house with a sad heart. Princess Moonlight was for him the most beautiful woman in the world; all others were dark beside her, and he thought of her night and day. His Majesty now spent much of his time in writing poems, telling her of his love and devotion, and sent them to her, and though she refused to see him again she answered with many verses of her own composing, which told him gently and kindly that she could never marry any one on this earth. These little songs always gave him pleasure.

At this time her foster-parents noticed that night after night the Princess would sit on her balcony and gaze for hours at the moon, in a spirit of the deepest dejection, ending always in a burst of tears. One night the old man found her thus weeping as if her heart were broken, and he besought her to tell him the reason of her sorrow.

With many tears she told him that he had guessed rightly when he supposed her not to belong to this world—that she had in truth come from the moon, and that her time on earth would soon be over. On the fifteenth day of that very month of August her friends from the moon would come to fetch her, and she would have to return. Her parents were both there, but having spent a lifetime on the earth she had forgotten them, and also the moon-world to which she belonged. It made her weep, she said, to think of leaving her kind foster-parents, and the home where she had been happy for so long.

When her attendants heard this they were very sad, and could not eat or drink for sadness at the thought that the Princess was so soon to leave them.

The Emperor, as soon as the news was carried to him, sent messengers to the house to find out if the report were true or not.

The old bamboo-cutter went out to meet the Imperial messengers. The last few days of sorrow had told upon the old man; he had aged greatly, and looked much more than his seventy years. Weeping bitterly, he told them that the report was only too true, but he intended, however, to make prisoners of the envoys from the moon, and to do all he could to prevent the Princess from being carried back.

The men returned and told His Majesty all that had passed. On the fifteenth day of that month the Emperor sent a guard of two thousand warriors to watch the house. One thousand stationed themselves on the roof, another thousand kept watch round all the entrances of the house. All were well trained archers, with bows and arrows. The bamboo-cutter and his wife hid Princess Moonlight in an inner room.

The old man gave orders that no one was to sleep that night, all in the house were to keep a strict watch, and be ready to protect the Princess. With these precautions, and the help of the Emperor's men-at-arms, he hoped to withstand the moon-messengers, but the Princess told him that all these measures to keep her would be useless, and that when her people came for her nothing whatever could prevent them from carrying out their purpose.

Even the Emperor's men would be powerless. Then she added with tears that she was very, very sorry to leave him and his wife, whom she had learned to love as her parents; that if she could do as she liked she would stay with them in their old age, and try to make some return for all the love and kindness they had showered upon her during all her earthly life.

The night wore on! The yellow harvest moon rose high in the heavens, flooding the world asleep with her golden light. Silence reigned over the pine and the bamboo forests, and on the roof where the thousand men-at-arms waited.

Then the night grew gray towards the dawn and all hoped that the danger was over—that Princess Moonlight would not have to leave them after all. Then suddenly the watchers saw a cloud form round the moon—and while they looked this cloud began to roll earthwards. Nearer and nearer it came, and every one saw with dismay that its course lay towards the house.

In a short time the sky was entirely obscured, till at last the cloud lay over the dwelling only ten feet off the ground. In the midst of the cloud there stood a flying chariot, and in the chariot a band of luminous beings. One amongst them who looked like a king and appeared to be the chief stepped out of the chariot, and, poised in air, called to the old man to come out.

"The time has come," he said, "for Princess Moonlight to return to the moon from whence she came. She committed a grave fault, and as a punishment was sent to live down here for a time. We know what good care you have taken of the Princess, and we have rewarded you for this and have sent you wealth and prosperity. We put the gold in the bamboos for you to find."

"I have brought up this Princess for twenty years and never once has she done a wrong thing, therefore the lady you are seeking cannot be this one," said the old man. "I pray you to look elsewhere."

Then the messenger called aloud, saying:

"Princess Moonlight, come out from this lowly dwelling. Rest not here another moment."

At these words the screens of the Princess's room slid open of their own accord, revealing the Princess shining in her own radiance, bright and wonderful and full of beauty.

The messenger led her forth and placed her in the chariot. She looked back, and saw with pity the deep sorrow of the old man. She spoke to him many comforting words, and told him that it was not her will to leave him and that he must always think of her when looking at the moon.

The bamboo-cutter implored to be allowed to accompany her, but this was not allowed. The Princess took off her embroidered outer garment and gave it to him as a keepsake.

One of the moon beings in the chariot held a wonderful coat of wings, another had a phial full of the Elixir of Life which was given the Princess to drink. She swallowed a little and was about to give the rest to the old man, but she was prevented from doing so.

The robe of wings was about to be put upon her shoulders, but she said:

"Wait a little. I must not forget my good friend the Emperor. I must write him once more to say good-by while still in this human form."

In spite of the impatience of the messengers and charioteers she kept them waiting while she wrote. She placed the phial of the Elixir of Life with the letter, and, giving them to the old man, she asked him to deliver them to the Emperor.

Then the chariot began to roll heavenwards towards the moon, and as they all gazed with tearful eyes at the receding Princess, the dawn broke, and in the rosy light of day the moon-chariot and all in it were lost amongst the fleecy clouds that were now wafted across the sky on the wings of the morning wind.

Princess Moonlight's letter was carried to the Palace. His Majesty was afraid to touch the Elixir of Life, so he sent it with the letter to the top of the most sacred mountain in the land, Mount Fuji, and there the Royal emissaries burnt it on the summit at sunrise. So to this day people say there is smoke to be seen rising from the top of Mount Fuji to the clouds.

GHOSTS AND MONSTERS

THE STORY of
MIMI-NASHI-HŌÏCHI

More than seven hundred years ago, at Dan-no-ura, in the Straits of Shimonoséki, was fought the last battle of the long contest between the Heiké, or Taira clan, and the Genji, or Minamoto clan. There the Heiké perished utterly, with their women and children, and their infant emperor likewise—now remembered as Antoku Tennō. And that sea and shore have been haunted for seven hundred years. . . . Elsewhere I told you about the strange crabs found there, called Heiké crabs, which have human faces on their backs, and are said to be the spirits of Heiké warriors.[1] But there are many strange things to be seen and heard along that coast. On dark nights thousands of ghostly fires hover about the beach, or flit above the waves,—pale lights which the fishermen call *Oni-bi*, or demon-fires; and, whenever the winds are up, a sound of great shouting comes from that sea, like a clamor of battle.

In former years the Heiké were much more restless than they now are. They would rise about ships passing in the night, and try to sink them; and at all times they would watch for swimmers, to pull them down. It was in order to appease those dead that the Buddhist temple, Amidaji, was built at

---

1.   See my *Kottō,* for a description of these curious crabs.

Akamagaséki.[2] A cemetery also was made close by, near the beach; and within it were set up monuments inscribed with the names of the drowned emperor and of his great vassals; and Buddhist services were regularly performed there, on behalf of the spirits of them. After the temple had been built, and the tombs erected, the Heiké gave less trouble than before; but they continued to do queer things at intervals,—proving that they had not found the perfect peace.

SOME CENTURIES AGO there lived at Akamagaséki a blind man named Hōïchi, who was famed for his skill in recitation and in playing upon the *biwa*.[3] From childhood he had been trained to recite and to play; and while yet a lad he had surpassed his teachers. As a professional *biwa-hōshi* he became famous chiefly by his recitations of the history of the Heiké and the Genji; and it is said that when he sang the song of the battle of Dan-no-ura "even the goblins [*kijin*] could not refrain from tears."

AT THE OUTSET of his career, Hōïchi was very poor; but he found a good friend to help him. The priest of the Amidaji was fond of poetry and music; and he often invited Hōïchi to the temple, to play and recite. Afterwards, being much impressed by the wonderful skill of the lad, the priest proposed that Hōïchi should make the temple his home; and this offer was gratefully accepted. Hōïchi was given a room in the temple-building; and, in return

---

2. Or, Shimonoséki. The town is also known by the name of Bakkan.

3. The *biwa*, a kind of four-stringed lute, is chiefly used in musical recitative. Formerly the professional minstrels who recited the *Heiké-Monogatari*, and other tragical histories, were called *biwa-hōshi*, or "lute-priests." The origin of this appellation is not clear; but it is possible that it may have been suggested by the fact that "lute-priests" as well as blind shampooers, had their heads shaven, like Buddhist priests. The *biwa* is played with a kind of plectrum, called *bachi*, usually made of horn.

for food and lodging, he was required only to gratify the priest with a musical performance on certain evenings, when otherwise disengaged.

ONE SUMMER NIGHT the priest was called away, to perform a Buddhist service at the house of a dead parishioner; and he went there with his acolyte, leaving Hōïchi alone in the temple. It was a hot night; and the blind man sought to cool himself on the verandah before his sleeping-room. The verandah overlooked a small garden in the rear of the Amidaji. There Hōïchi waited for the priest's return, and tried to relieve his solitude by practicing upon his *biwa*. Midnight passed; and the priest did not appear. But the atmosphere was still too warm for comfort within doors; and Hōïchi remained outside. At last he heard steps approaching from the back gate. Somebody crossed the garden, advanced to the verandah, and halted directly in front of him—but it was not the priest. A deep voice called the blind man's name—abruptly and unceremoniously, in the manner of a samurai summoning an inferior:—

"Hōïchi!"

Hōïchi was too much startled, for the moment, to respond: and the voice called again, in a tone of harsh command,—

"Hōïchi!"

"*Hai!*" answered the blind man, frightened by the menace in the voice,—"I am blind!—I cannot know who calls!"

"There is nothing to fear," the stranger exclaimed, speaking more gently. "I am stopping near this temple, and have been sent to you with a message. My present lord, a person of exceedingly high rank, is now staying in Akamagaséki, with many noble attendants. He wished to view the scene of the battle of Dan-no-ura; and to-day he visited that place. Having heard of your skill in reciting the story of the battle, he now desires to hear your performance: so you will take your *biwa* and come with me at once to the house where the august assembly is waiting."

In those times, the order of a samurai was not to be lightly disobeyed. Hōï-chi donned his sandals, took his *biwa*, and went away with the stranger, who guided him deftly, but obliged him to walk very fast. The hand that guided was iron; and the clank of the warrior's stride proved him fully armed,—probably some palace-guard on duty. Hōïchi's first alarm was over: he began to imagine himself in good luck;—for, remembering the retainer's assurance about a "person of exceedingly high rank," he thought that the lord who wished to hear the recitation could not be less than a daimyō of the first class. Presently the samurai halted; and Hōïchi became aware that they had arrived at a large gateway;—and he wondered, for he could not remember any large gate in that part of the town, except the main gate of the Amidaji. "*Kaimon!*"[4] the samurai called,—and there was a sound of unbarring; and the twain passed on. They traversed a space of garden, and halted again before some entrance; and the retainer cried in a loud voice, "Within there! I have brought Hōïchi." Then came sounds of feet hurrying, and screens sliding, and rain-doors opening, and voices of women in converse. By the language of the women Hōïchi knew them to be domestics in some noble household; but he could not imagine to what place he had been conducted. Little time was allowed him for conjecture. After he had been helped to mount several stone steps, upon the last of which he was told to leave his sandals, a woman's hand guided him along interminable reaches of polished planking, and round pillared angles too many to remember, and over widths amazing of matted floor,—into the middle of some vast apartment. There he thought that many great people were assembled: the sound of the rustling of silk was like the sound of leaves in a forest. He heard also a great humming of voices,—talking in undertones; and the speech was the speech of courts.

Hōïchi was told to put himself at ease, and he found a kneeling-cushion ready for him. After having taken his place upon it, and tuned his instru-

---

4. A respectful term, signifying the opening of a gate. It was used by samurai when calling to the guards on duty at a lord's gate for admission.

ment, the voice of a woman—whom he divined to be the *Rōjo*, or matron in charge of the female service—addressed him, saying,—

"It is now required that the history of the Heiké be recited, to the accompaniment of the *biwa*."

Now the entire recital would have required a time of many nights: therefore Hōïchi ventured a question:—

"As the whole of the story is not soon told, what portion is it augustly desired that I now recite?"

The woman's voice made answer:—

"Recite the story of the battle at Dan-no-ura,—for the pity of it is the most deep."[5]

Then Hōïchi lifted up his voice, and chanted the chant of the fight on the bitter sea,—wonderfully making his *biwa* to sound like the straining of oars and the rushing of ships, the whirr and the hissing of arrows, the shouting and trampling of men, the crashing of steel upon helmets, the plunging of slain in the flood. And to left and right of him, in the pauses of his playing, he could hear voices murmuring praise: "How marvelous an artist!"—"Never in our own province was playing heard like this!"—"Not in all the empire is there another singer like Hōïchi!" Then fresh courage came to him, and he played and sang yet better than before; and a hush of wonder deepened about him. But when at last he came to tell the fate of the fair and helpless,—the piteous perishing of the women and children,—and the death-leap of Nii-no-Ama, with the imperial infant in her arms,—then all the listeners uttered together one long, long shuddering cry of anguish; and thereafter they wept and wailed so loudly and so wildly that the blind man was frightened by the violence and grief that he had made. For much time the sobbing and the wailing continued. But gradually the sounds of

---

5.   Or the phrase might be rendered, "for the pity of that part is the deepest." The Japanese word for pity in the original text is *awaré*.

lamentation died away; and again, in the great stillness that followed, Hōï-chi heard the voice of the woman whom he supposed to be the Rōjo.

She said:—

"Although we had been assured that you were a very skillful player upon the *biwa*, and without an equal in recitative, we did not know that any one could be so skillful as you have proved yourself to-night. Our lord has been pleased to say that he intends to bestow upon you a fitting reward. But he desires that you shall perform before him once every night for the next six nights— after which time he will probably make his august return-journey. To-morrow night, therefore, you are to come here at the same hour. The retainer who to-night conducted you will be sent for you . . . There is another matter about which I have been ordered to inform you. It is required that you shall speak to no one of your visits here, during the time of our lord's august sojourn at Akamagaséki. As he is traveling incognito,[6] he commands that no mention of these things be made . . . You are now free to go back to your temple."

AFTER HŌÏCHI had duly expressed his thanks, a woman's hand conducted him to the entrance of the house, where the same retainer, who had before guided him, was waiting to take him home. The retainer led him to the verandah at the rear of the temple, and there bade him farewell.

IT WAS ALMOST DAWN when Hōïchi returned; but his absence from the temple had not been observed,—as the priest, coming back at a very late hour, had supposed him asleep. During the day Hōïchi was able to take some rest; and he said nothing about his strange adventure. In the middle

---

6.   "Traveling incognito" is at least the meaning of the original phrase,—"making a disguised august journey" *(shinobi no go-ryokō)*.

of the following night the samurai again came for him, and led him to the august assembly, where he gave another recitation with the same success that had attended his previous performance. But during this second visit his absence from the temple was accidentally discovered; and after his return in the morning he was summoned to the presence of the priest, who said to him, in a tone of kindly reproach:—

"We have been very anxious about you, friend Hōïchi. To go out, blind and alone, at so late an hour, is dangerous. Why did you go without telling us? I could have ordered a servant to accompany you. And where have you been?"

Hōïchi answered, evasively,—

"Pardon me, kind friend! I had to attend to some private business; and I could not arrange the matter at any other hour."

The priest was surprised, rather than pained, by Hōïchi's reticence: he felt it to be unnatural, and suspected something wrong. He feared that the blind lad had been bewitched or deluded by some evil spirits. He did not ask any more questions; but he privately instructed the men-servants of the temple to keep watch upon Hōïchi's movements, and to follow him in case that he should again leave the temple after dark.

ON THE VERY NEXT NIGHT, Hōïchi was seen to leave the temple; and the servants immediately lighted their lanterns, and followed after him. But it was a rainy night, and very dark; and before the temple-folks could get to the roadway, Hōïchi had disappeared. Evidently he had walked very fast,—a strange thing, considering his blindness; for the road was in a bad condition. The men hurried through the streets, making inquiries at every house which Hōïchi was accustomed to visit; but nobody could give them any news of him. At last, as they were returning to the temple by way of the shore, they were startled by the sound of a biwa, furiously played, in the cemetery of the Amidaji. Except for some ghostly fires—such as usually flitted there on dark nights—all was blackness in that direction. But the men at once hastened to the cemetery; and there, by the help of their lanterns, they discovered Hōïchi,—sitting alone in the rain before the memorial tomb of Antoku Tennō, making his *biwa* resound, and loudly chanting the chant of the battle of Dan-no-ura. And behind him, and about him, and everywhere above the tombs, the fires of the dead were burning, like candles. Never before had so great a host of *Oni-bi* appeared in the sight of mortal man . . .

"Hōïchi San!—Hōïchi San!" the servants cried,—"you are bewitched! . . . Hōïchi San!"

But the blind man did not seem to hear. Strenuously he made his biwa to rattle and ring and clang;—more and more wildly he chanted the chant of the battle of Dan-no-ura. They caught hold of him;—they shouted into his ear,—

"Hōïchi San!—Hōïchi San!—come home with us at once!"

Reprovingly he spoke to them:—

"To interrupt me in such a manner, before this august assembly, will not be tolerated."

Whereat, in spite of the weirdness of the thing, the servants could not help laughing. Sure that he had been bewitched, they now seized him, and pulled him up on his feet, and by main force hurried him back to the temple,—where he was immediately relieved of his wet clothes, by order of the priest, and reclad, and made to eat and drink. Then the priest insisted upon a full explanation of his friend's astonishing behavior.

Hōïchi long hesitated to speak. But at last, finding that his conduct had really alarmed and angered the good priest, he decided to abandon his reserve; and he related everything that had happened from the time of first visit of the samurai.

The priest said:—

"Hōïchi, my poor friend, you are now in great danger! How unfortunate that you did not tell me all this before! Your wonderful skill in music has indeed brought you into strange trouble. By this time you must be aware that you have not been visiting any house whatever, but have been passing your nights in the cemetery, among the tombs of the Heiké;—and it was before the memorial-tomb of Antoku Tennō that our people to-night found you, sitting in the rain. All that you have been imagining was illusion—except the calling of the dead. By once obeying them, you have put yourself in their power. If you obey them again, after what has already occurred, they will tear you in pieces. But they would have destroyed you, sooner or later, in any event. . . . Now I shall not be able to remain with you to-night: I am called away to perform another service. But, before I go, it will be necessary to protect your body by writing holy texts upon it."

BEFORE SUNDOWN the priest and his acolyte stripped Hōïchi: then, with their writing-brushes, they traced upon his breast and back, head and face and neck, limbs and hands and feet,—even upon the soles of his feet, and upon all parts of his body,—the text of the holy sûtra called *Hannya-Shin-Kyō*.[7] When this had been done, the priest instructed Hōïchi, saying:—

"To-night, as soon as I go away, you must seat yourself on the verandah, and wait. You will be called. But, whatever may happen, do not answer, and do not move. Say nothing and sit still—as if meditating. If you stir, or make any noise, you will be torn asunder. Do not get frightened; and do not think of calling for help—because no help could save you. If you do exactly as I tell you, the danger will pass, and you will have nothing more to fear."

---

7.   The Smaller Pragña-Pâramitâ-Hridaya-Sûtra is thus called in Japanese. Both the smaller and larger sûtras called Pragña-Pâramitâ ("Transcendent Wisdom") have been translated by the late Professor Max Müller, and can be found in volume xlix. of the *Sacred Books of the East* ("Buddhist Mahâyâna Sûtras").—Apropos of the magical use of the text, as described in this story, it is worth remarking that the subject of the sûtra is the Doctrine of the Emptiness of Forms,— that is to say, of the unreal character of all phenomena or noumena. . . . "Form is emptiness; and emptiness is form. Emptiness is not different from form; form is not different from emptiness. What is form—that is emptiness. What is emptiness—that is form. . . . Perception, name, concept, and knowledge, are also emptiness. . . . There is no eye, ear, nose, tongue, body, and mind. . . . But when the envelopment of consciousness has been annihilated, then he [*the seeker*] becomes free from all fear, and beyond the reach of change, enjoying final Nirvâna."

AFTER DARK the priest and the acolyte went away; and Hōïchi seated himself on the verandah, according to the instructions given him. He laid his *biwa* on the planking beside him, and, assuming the attitude of meditation, remained quite still,—taking care not to cough, or to breathe audibly. For hours he stayed thus.

Then, from the roadway, he heard the steps coming. They passed the gate, crossed the garden, approached the verandah, stopped—directly in front of him.

"Hōïchi!" the deep voice called. But the blind man held his breath, and sat motionless.

"Hōïchi!" grimly called the voice a second time. Then a third time—savagely:—

"Hōïchi!"

Hōïchi remained as still as a stone,—and the voice grumbled:—

"No answer!—that won't do! . . . Must see where the fellow is." . . .

There was a noise of heavy feet mounting upon the verandah. The feet approached deliberately,—halted beside him. Then, for long minutes,—during which Hōïchi felt his whole body shake to the beating of his heart,—there was dead silence.

At last the gruff voice muttered close to him:—

"Here is the *biwa*; but of the *biwa*-player I see—only two ears! . . . So that explains why he did not answer: he had no mouth to answer with—there is nothing left of him but his ears. . . . Now to my lord those ears I will take—in proof that the august commands have been obeyed, so far as was possible" . . .

At that instant Hōïchi felt his ears gripped by fingers of iron, and torn off! Great as the pain was, he gave no cry. The heavy footfalls receded along the verandah,—descended into the garden,—passed out to the roadway,—ceased. From either side of his head, the blind man felt a thick warm trickling; but he dared not lift his hands. . . .

BEFORE SUNRISE the priest came back. He hastened at once to the verandah in the rear, stepped and slipped upon something clammy, and uttered a cry of horror;—for he saw, by the light of his lantern, that the clamminess was blood. But he perceived Hōïchi sitting there, in the attitude of meditation—with the blood still oozing from his wounds.

"My poor Hōïchi!" cried the startled priest,—"what is this?…You have been hurt?"

At the sound of his friend's voice, the blind man felt safe. He burst out sobbing, and tearfully told his adventure of the night.

"Poor, poor Hōïchi!" the priest exclaimed,—"all my fault!—my very grievous fault!…Everywhere upon your body the holy texts had been written—except upon your ears! I trusted my acolyte to do that part of the work; and it was very, very wrong of me not to have made sure that he had done it!…Well, the matter cannot now be helped;—we can only try to heal your hurts as soon as possible.…Cheer up, friend!—the danger is now well over. You will never again be troubled by those visitors."

WITH THE AID of a good doctor, Hōïchi soon recovered from his injuries. The story of his strange adventure spread far and wide, and soon made him famous. Many noble persons went to Akamagaséki to hear him recite; and large presents of money were given to him,—so that he became a wealthy man.…But from the time of his adventure, he was known only by the appellation of *Mimi-nashi-Hōïchi*: "Hōïchi-the-Earless."

YUKI-ONNA

In a village of Musashi Province, there lived two woodcutters: Mosaku and Minokichi. At the time of which I am speaking, Mosaku was an old man; and Minokichi, his apprentice, was a lad of eighteen years. Every day they went together to a forest situated about five miles from their village. On the way to that forest there is a wide river to cross; and there is a ferry-boat. Several times a bridge was built where the ferry is; but the bridge was each time carried away by a flood. No common bridge can resist the current there when the river rises.

Mosaku and Minokichi were on their way home, one very cold evening, when a great snowstorm overtook them. They reached the ferry; and they found that the boatman had gone away, leaving his boat on the other side of the river. It was no day for swimming; and the woodcutters took shelter in the ferryman's hut,—thinking themselves lucky to find any shelter at all. There was no brazier in the hut, nor any place in which to make a fire: it was only a two-mat[1] hut, with a single door, but no window. Mosaku and Minokichi fastened the door, and lay down to rest, with their straw rain-coats over them. At first they did not feel very cold; and they thought that the storm would soon be over.

---

1.   That is to say, with a floor-surface of about six feet square.

The old man almost immediately fell asleep; but the boy, Minokichi, lay awake a long time, listening to the awful wind, and the continual slashing of the snow against the door. The river was roaring; and the hut swayed and creaked like a junk at sea. It was a terrible storm; and the air was every moment becoming colder; and Minokichi shivered under his rain-coat. But at last, in spite of the cold, he too fell asleep.

He was awakened by a showering of snow in his face. The door of the hut had been forced open; and, by the snow-light (*yuki-akari*), he saw a woman in the room,—a woman all in white. She was bending above Mosaku, and blowing her breath upon him;—and her breath was like a bright white smoke. Almost in the same moment she turned to Minokichi, and stooped over him. He tried to cry out, but found that he could not utter any sound. The white woman bent down over him, lower and lower, until her face almost touched him; and he saw that she was very beautiful,— though her eyes made him afraid. For a little time she continued to look at him;—then she smiled, and she whispered:—"I intended to treat you like the other man. But I cannot help feeling some pity for you,—because you are so young. . . . You are a pretty boy, Minokichi; and I will not hurt you now. But, if you ever tell anybody—even your own mother—about what you have seen this night, I shall know it; and then I will kill you. . . . Remember what I say!"

With these words, she turned from him, and passed through the doorway. Then he found himself able to move; and he sprang up, and looked out. But the woman was nowhere to be seen; and the snow was driving furiously into the hut. Minokichi closed the door, and secured it by fixing several billets of wood against it. He wondered if the wind had blown it open;—he thought that he might have been only dreaming, and might have mistaken the gleam of the snow-light in the doorway for the figure of a white woman: but he could not be sure. He called to Mosaku, and was frightened because the old man did not answer. He put out his hand in the dark, and touched Mosaku's face, and found that it was ice! Mosaku was stark and dead. . . .

BY DAWN the storm was over; and when the ferryman returned to his station, a little after sunrise, he found Minokichi lying senseless beside the frozen body of Mosaku. Minokichi was promptly cared for, and soon came to himself; but he remained a long time ill from the effects of the cold of that terrible night. He had been greatly frightened also by the old man's death; but he said nothing about the vision of the woman in white. As soon as he got well again, he returned to his calling,—going alone every morning to the forest, and coming back at nightfall with his bundles of wood, which his mother helped him to sell.

ONE EVENING, in the winter of the following year, as he was on his way home, he overtook a girl who happened to be traveling by the same road. She was a tall, slim girl, very good-looking; and she answered Minokichi's greeting in a voice as pleasant to the ear as the voice of a song-bird. Then he walked beside her; and they began to talk. The girl said that her name was O-Yuki[2]; that she had lately lost both of her parents; and that she was going to Yedo, where she happened to have some poor relations, who might help her to find a situation as a servant. Minokichi soon felt charmed by this strange girl; and the more that he looked at her, the handsomer she appeared to be. He asked her whether she was yet betrothed; and she answered, laughingly, that she was free. Then, in her turn, she asked Minokichi whether he was married, or pledged to marry; and he told her that, although he had

---

2.   This name, signifying "Snow," is not uncommon. On the subject of Japanese female names, see my paper in the volume entitled *Shadowings*.

only a widowed mother to support, the question of an "honorable daughter-in-law" had not yet been considered, as he was very young. . . . After these confidences, they walked on for a long while without speaking; but, as the proverb declares, *Ki ga aréba, mé mo kuchi hodo ni mono wo iu*: "When the wish is there, the eyes can say as much as the mouth." By the time they reached the village, they had become very much pleased with each other; and then Minokichi asked O-Yuki to rest awhile at his house. After some shy hesitation, she went there with him; and his mother made her welcome, and prepared a warm meal for her. O-Yuki behaved so nicely that Minokichi's mother took a sudden fancy to her, and persuaded her to delay her journey to Yedo. And the natural end of the matter was that Yuki never went to Yedo at all. She remained in the house, as an "honorable daughter-in-law."

O-YUKI PROVED a very good daughter-in-law. When Minokichi's mother came to die,—some five years later,—her last words were words of affection and praise for the wife of her son. And O-Yuki bore Minokichi ten children, boys and girls,—handsome children all of them, and very fair of skin.

The country-folk thought O-Yuki a wonderful person, by nature different from themselves. Most of the peasant-women age early; but O-Yuki, even after having become the mother of ten children, looked as young and fresh as on the day when she had first come to the village.

ONE NIGHT, after the children had gone to sleep, O-Yuki was sewing by the light of a paper lamp; and Minokichi, watching her, said:—

"To see you sewing there, with the light on your face, makes me think of a strange thing that happened when I was a lad of eighteen. I then saw somebody as beautiful and white as you are now—indeed, she was very like you." . . .

Without lifting her eyes from her work, O-Yuki responded:—

"Tell me about her. . . . Where did you see her?"

Then Minokichi told her about the terrible night in the ferryman's hut,—and about the White Woman that had stooped above him, smiling and whispering,—and about the silent death of old Mosaku. And he said:—

"Asleep or awake, that was the only time that I saw a being as beautiful as you. Of course, she was not a human being; and I was afraid of her,— very much afraid,—but she was so white! . . . Indeed, I have never been sure whether it was a dream that I saw, or the Woman of the Snow.". . .

O-Yuki flung down her sewing, and arose, and bowed above Minokichi where he sat, and shrieked into his face:—

"It was I—I—I! Yuki it was! And I told you then that I would kill you if you ever said one word about it! . . . But for those children asleep there, I would kill you this moment! And now you had better take very, very good care of them; for if ever they have reason to complain of you, I will treat you as you deserve!". . .

Even as she screamed, her voice became thin, like a crying of wind;— then she melted into a bright white mist that spired to the roof-beams, and shuddered away through the smoke-hold . . . Never again was she seen.

DIPLOMACY

It had been ordered that the execution should take place in the garden of the *yashiki*. So the man was taken there, and made to kneel down in a wide sanded space crossed by a line of *tobi-ishi*, or stepping-stones, such as you may still see in Japanese landscape-gardens. His arms were bound behind him. Retainers brought water in buckets, and rice-bags filled with pebbles; and they packed the rice-bags round the kneeling man,—so wedging him in that he could not move. The master came, and observed the arrangements. He found them satisfactory, and made no remarks.

Suddenly the condemned man cried out to him:—

"Honored Sir, the fault for which I have been doomed I did not wittingly commit. It was only my very great stupidity which caused the fault. Having been born stupid, by reason of my Karma, I could not always help making mistakes. But to kill a man for being stupid is wrong,—and that wrong will be repaid. So surely as you kill me, so surely shall I be avenged;—out of the resentment that you provoke will come the vengeance; and evil will be rendered for evil." . . .

If any person be killed while feeling strong resentment, the ghost of that person will be able to take vengeance upon the killer. This the samurai knew. He replied very gently,—almost caressingly:—

"We shall allow you to frighten us as much as you please—after you are dead. But it is difficult to believe that you mean what you say. Will you try to give us some sign of your great resentment—after your head has been cut off?"

"Assuredly I will," answered the man.

"Very well," said the samurai, drawing his long sword;—"I am now going to cut off your head. Directly in front of you there is a stepping-stone. After your head has been cut off, try to bite the stepping-stone. If your angry ghost can help you to do that, some of us may be frightened. …Will you try to bite the stone?"

"I will bite it!" cried the man, in great anger,—"I will bite it!—I will bite"—

There was a flash, a swish, a crunching thud: the bound body bowed over the rice sacks,—two long blood-jets pumping from the shorn neck;— and the head rolled upon the sand. Heavily toward the stepping-stone it rolled: then, suddenly bounding, it caught the upper edge of the stone between its teeth, clung desperately for a moment, and dropped inert.

NONE SPOKE; but the retainers stared in horror at their master. He seemed to be quite unconcerned. He merely held out his sword to the nearest attendant, who, with a wooden dipper, poured water over the blade from haft to point, and then carefully wiped the steel several times with sheets of soft paper. … And thus ended the ceremonial part of the incident.

FOR MONTHS THEREAFTER, the retainers and the domestics lived in ceaseless fear of ghostly visitation. None of them doubted that the prom- ised vengeance would come; and their constant terror caused them to hear and to see much that did not exist. They became afraid of the sound of the wind in the bamboos,—afraid even of the stirring of shadows in the garden. At last, after taking counsel together, they decided to petition their master to have a *Ségaki*-service performed on behalf of the vengeful spirit.

"Quite unnecessary," the samurai said, when his chief retainer had uttered the general wish.…"I understand that the desire of a dying man for revenge may be a cause for fear. But in this case there is nothing to fear."

The retainer looked at his master beseechingly, but hesitated to ask the reason of the alarming confidence.

"Oh, the reason is simple enough," declared the samurai, divining the unspoken doubt. "Only the very last intention of the fellow could have been dangerous; and when I challenged him to give me the sign, I diverted his mind from the desire of revenge. He died with the set purpose of biting the stepping-stone; and that purpose he was able to accomplish, but nothing else. All the rest he must have forgotten.… So you need not feel any further anxiety about the matter."

—And indeed the dead man gave no more trouble. Nothing at all happened.

MUJINA

On the Akasaka Road, in Tōkyō, there is a slope called Kii-no-kuni-zaka,—which means the Slope of the Province of Kii. I do not know why it is called the Slope of the Province of Kii. On one side of this slope you see an ancient moat, deep and very wide, with high green banks rising up to some place of gardens;—and on the other side of the road extend the long and lofty walls of an imperial palace. Before the era of street-lamps and jinrikishas, this neighborhood was very lonesome after dark; and belated pedestrians would go miles out of their way rather than mount the Kii-no-kuni-zaka, alone, after sunset.

All because of a Mujina that used to walk there.

THE LAST MAN who saw the Mujina was an old merchant of the Kyōbashi quarter, who died about thirty years ago. This is the story, as he told it:—

One night, at a late hour, he was hurrying up the Kii-no-kuni-zaka, when he perceived a woman crouching by the moat, all alone, and weeping bitterly. Fearing that she intended to drown herself, he stopped to offer her any assistance or consolation in his power. She appeared to be a slight and graceful person, handsomely dressed; and her hair was arranged like that of a young girl of good family. "O-jochū[1]," he exclaimed, approaching her,—"O-jochū, do not cry like that! . . . Tell me what the trouble is; and if there be any way to help you, I shall be glad to help you." (He really meant what he said; for he was a very kind man.) But she continued to weep,—hiding her face from him with one of her long sleeves. "O-jochū," he said again, as gently as he could,—"please, please listen to me! . . . This is no place for a young lady at night! Do not cry, I implore you!—only tell me how I may be of some help to you!" Slowly she rose up, but turned her back to him, and continued to moan and sob behind her sleeve. He laid his hand lightly upon her shoulder, and pleaded:—"O-jochū!—O-jochū!—O-jochū!…Listen to me, just for one little moment! . . . O-jochū!—O-jochū!" …Then that O-jochū turned around, and dropped her sleeve, and stroked her face with her hand;—and the man saw that she had no eyes or nose or mouth,—and he screamed and ran away.

Up Kii-no-kuni-zaka he ran and ran; and all was black and empty before him. On and on he ran, never daring to look back; and at last he saw a lantern, so far away that it looked like the gleam of a firefly; and he made for it. It proved to be only the lantern of an itinerant *soba*-seller,[2] who had set down his stand by the road-side; but any light and any human companionship was good after that experience; and he flung himself down at the feet of the *soba*-seller, crying out, "Aa!—aa!!—*aa!!!*" . . .

"*Koré! koré!*" roughly exclaimed the soba-man. "Here! what is the matter with you? Anybody hurt you?"

"No—nobody hurt me," panted the other,—"only . . . *Aa!—aa!*" . . .

"—Only scared you?" queried the peddler, unsympathetically. "Robbers?"

"Not robbers,—not robbers," gasped the terrified man. . . . "I saw . . . I

---

1.   O-jochū ("honorable damsel"), – a polite form of adress used in speaking to a young lady whom one does not know.

2.   *Soba* is a preparation of buckwheat, somewhat resembling vermicelli.

saw a woman—by the moat;—and she showed me. . . *Aa!* I cannot tell you what she showed me!"...

"*Hé!* Was it anything like THIS that she showed you?" cried the *soba*-man, stroking his own face—which therewith became like unto an Egg.... And, simultaneously, the light went out.

A DEAD SECRET

A long time ago, in the province of Tamba, there lived a rich merchant named Inamuraya Gensuké. He had a daughter called O-Sono. As she was very clever and pretty, he thought it would be a pity to let her grow up with only such teaching as the country-teachers could give her: so he sent her, in care of some trusty attendants, to Kyōto, that she might be trained in the polite accomplishments taught to the ladies of the capital. After she had thus been educated, she was married to a friend of her father's family—a merchant named Nagaraya;—and she lived happily with him for nearly four years. They had one child,—a boy. But O-Sono fell ill and died, in the fourth year after her marriage.

On the night after the funeral of O-Sono, her little son said that his mamma had come back, and was in the room upstairs. She had smiled at him, but would not talk to him: so he became afraid, and ran away. Then some of the family went upstairs to the room which had been O-Sono's; and they were startled to see, by the light of a small lamp which had been kindled before a shrine in that room, the figure of the dead mother. She appeared as if standing in front of a *tansu*, or chest of drawers, that still contained her ornaments and her wearing-apparel. Her head and shoulders could be very distinctly seen; but from the waist downwards the figure thinned into invisibility;—it was like an imperfect reflection of her, and transparent as a shadow on water.

Then the folk were afraid, and left the room. Below they consulted together; and the mother of O-Sono's husband said: "A woman is fond of her small things; and O-Sono was much attached to her belongings. Perhaps she has come back to look at them. Many dead persons will do that,— unless the things be given to the parish-temple. If we present O-Sono's robes and girdles to the temple, her spirit will probably find rest."

It was agreed that this should be done as soon as possible. So on the following morning the drawers were emptied; and all of O-Sono's ornaments and dresses were taken to the temple. But she came back the next night, and looked at the *tansu* as before. And she came back also on the night following, and the night after that, and every night;—and the house became a house of fear.

THE MOTHER of O-Sono's husband then went to the parish-temple, and told the chief priest all that had happened, and asked for ghostly counsel. The temple was a Zen temple; and the head-priest was a learned old man, known as Daigen Oshō. He said: "There must be something about which she is anxious, in or near that *tansu*."—"But we emptied all the drawers," replied the woman;—"there is nothing in the *tansu*."—"Well," said Daigen Oshō, "to-night I shall go to your house, and keep watch in that room, and see what can be done. You must give orders that no person shall enter the room while I am watching, unless I call."

After sundown, Daigen Oshō went to the house, and found the room made ready for him. He remained there alone, reading the sûtras; and nothing appeared until after the Hour of the Rat.[1] Then the figure of O-Sono suddenly outlined itself in front of the *tansu*. Her face had a wistful look; and she kept her eyes fixed upon the *tansu*.

---

1. The Hour of the Rat *(Né-no-Koku)*, according to the old Japanese method of reckoning time, was the first hour. It corresponded to the time between our midnight and two o'clock in the morning; for the ancient Japanese hours were each equal to two modern hours.

The priest uttered the holy formula prescribed in such cases, and then, addressing the figure by the *kaimyō*[2] of O-Sono, said:—"I have come here in order to help you. Perhaps in that *tansu* there is something about which you have reason to feel anxious. Shall I try to find it for you?" The shadow appeared to give assent by a slight motion of the head; and the priest, rising, opened the top drawer. It was empty. Successively he opened the second, the third, and the fourth drawer;—he searched carefully behind them and beneath them;—he carefully examined the interior of the chest. He found nothing. But the figure remained gazing as wistfully as before. "What can she want?" thought the priest. Suddenly it occurred to him that there might be something hidden under the paper with which the drawers were lined. He removed the lining of the first drawer:—nothing! He removed the lining of the second and third drawers:—still nothing. But under the lining of the lowermost drawer he found—a letter. "Is this the thing about which you have been troubled?" he asked. The shadow of the woman turned toward him,—her faint gaze fixed upon the letter. "Shall I burn it for you?" he asked. She bowed before him. "It shall be burned in the temple this very morning," he promised;—"and no one shall read it, except myself." The figure smiled and vanished.

DAWN WAS BREAKING as the priest descended the stairs, to find the family waiting anxiously below. "Do not be anxious," he said to them: "She will not appear again." And she never did.

The letter was burned. It was a love-letter written to O-Sono in the time of her studies at Kyōto. But the priest alone knew what was in it; and the secret died with him.

---

2. *Kaimyō*, the posthumous Buddhist name, or religious name, given to the dead. Strictly speaking, the meaning of the word is silâ-name. (See my paper entitled "The Literature of the Dead" in *Exotics and Retrospectives*.)

ROKURO-KUBI

Nearly five hundred years ago there was a samurai, named Isogai Héïdazaëmon Takétsura, in the service of the Lord Kikuji, of Kyūshū. This Isogai had inherited, from many warlike ancestors, a natural aptitude for military exercises, and extraordinary strength. While yet a boy he had surpassed his teachers in the art of swordsmanship, in archery, and in the use of the spear, and had displayed all the capacities of a daring and skillful soldier. Afterwards, in the time of the Eikyō[1] war, he so distinguished himself that high honors were bestowed upon him. But when the house of Kikuji came to ruin, Isogai found himself without a master. He might then easily have obtained service under another daimyō; but as he had never sought distinction for his own sake alone, and as his heart remained true to his former lord, he preferred to give up the world. So he cut off his hair, and became a traveling priest,—taking the Buddhist name of Kwairyō.

But always, under the *koromo*[2] of the priest, Kwairyō kept warm within him the heart of the samurai. As in other years he had laughed at peril, so

---

1.   The period of Eikyō lasted from 1429 to 1441.

2.   The upper robe of a Buddhist priest is thus called.

now also he scorned danger; and in all weathers and all seasons he journeyed to preach the good Law in places where no other priest would have dared to go. For that age was an age of violence and disorder; and upon the highways there was no security for the solitary traveler, even if he happened to be a priest.

In the course of his first long journey, Kwairyō had occasion to visit the province of Kai. One evening, as he was traveling through the mountains of that province, darkness overcame him in a very lonesome district, leagues away from any village. So he resigned himself to pass the night under the stars; and having found a suitable grassy spot, by the roadside, he lay down there, and prepared to sleep. He had always welcomed discomfort; and even a bare rock was for him a good bed, when nothing better could be found, and the root of a pine-tree an excellent pillow. His body was iron; and he never troubled himself about dews or rain or frost or snow.

Scarcely had he lain down when a man came along the road, carrying an axe and a great bundle of chopped wood. This woodcutter halted on seeing Kwairyō lying down, and, after a moment of silent observation, said to him in a tone of great surprise:—

"What kind of a man can you be, good Sir, that you dare to lie down alone in such a place as this?... There are haunters about here,—many of them. Are you not afraid of Hairy Things?"

"My friend," cheerfully answered Kwairyō, "I am only a wandering priest,—a 'Cloud-and-Water-Guest,' as folks call it: *Unsui-no-ryokaku*. And I am not in the least afraid of Hairy Things,—if you mean goblin-foxes, or goblin-badgers, or any creatures of that kind. As for lonesome places, I like them: they are suitable for meditation. I am accustomed to sleeping in the open air: and I have learned never to be anxious about my life."

"You must be indeed a brave man, Sir Priest," the peasant responded, "to lie down here! This place has a bad name,—a very bad name. But, as the proverb has it, *Kunshi ayayuki ni chikayorazu* ['The superior man does not needlessly expose himself to peril']; and I must assure you, Sir, that it is very dangerous to sleep here. Therefore, although my house is only a wretched thatched hut, let me beg of you to come home with me at once. In the way of food, I have nothing to offer you; but there is a roof at least, and you can sleep under it without risk."

He spoke earnestly; and Kwairyō, liking the kindly tone of the man, accepted this modest offer. The woodcutter guided him along a narrow path, leading up from the main road through mountain-forest. It was a rough and dangerous path,—sometimes skirting precipices,—sometimes offering nothing but a network of slippery roots for the foot to rest upon,—sometimes winding over or between masses of jagged rock. But at last Kwairyō found himself upon a cleared space at the top of a hill, with a full moon shining overhead; and he saw before him a small thatched cottage, cheerfully lighted from within. The woodcutter led him to a shed at the back of the house, whither water had been conducted, through bamboo-pipes, from some neighboring stream; and the two men washed their feet. Beyond the shed was a vegetable garden, and a grove of cedars and bamboos; and beyond the trees appeared the glimmer of a cascade, pouring from some loftier height, and swaying in the moonshine like a long white robe.

As Kwairyō entered the cottage with his guide, he perceived four persons—men and women—warming their hands at a little fire kindled in the *ro*[3] of the principle apartment. They bowed low to the priest, and greeted him in the most respectful manner. Kwairyō wondered that persons so poor, and

---

3. A sort of little fireplace, contrived in the floor of a room, is thus described. The *ro* is usually a square shallow cavity, lined with metal and half-filled with ashes, in which charcoal is lighted.

dwelling in such a solitude, should be aware of the polite forms of greeting. "These are good people," he thought to himself; "and they must have been taught by some one well acquainted with the rules of propriety." Then turning to his host,—the *aruji*, or house-master, as the others called him,—Kwairyō said:—

"From the kindness of your speech, and from the very polite welcome given me by your household, I imagine that you have not always been a woodcutter. Perhaps you formerly belonged to one of the upper classes?"

Smiling, the woodcutter answered:—

"Sir, you are not mistaken. Though now living as you find me, I was once a person of some distinction. My story is the story of a ruined life—ruined by my own fault. I used to be in the service of a daimyō; and my rank in that service was not inconsiderable. But I loved women and wine too well; and under the influence of passion I acted wickedly. My selfishness brought about the ruin of our house, and caused the death of many persons. Retribution followed me; and I long remained a fugitive in the land. Now I often pray that I may be able to make some atonement for the evil which I did, and to reestablish the ancestral home. But I fear that I shall never find any way of so doing. Nevertheless, I try to overcome the karma of my errors by sincere repentance, and by helping as far as I can, those who are unfortunate."

Kwairyō was pleased by this announcement of good resolve; and he said to the *aruji*:—

"My friend, I have had occasion to observe that man, prone to folly in their youth, may in after years become very earnest in right living. In the holy sûtras it is written that those strongest in wrong-doing can become, by power of good resolve, the strongest in right-doing. I do not doubt that you have a good heart; and I hope that better fortune will come to you. To-night I shall recite the sûtras for your sake, and pray that you may obtain the force to overcome the karma of any past errors."

With these assurances, Kwairyō bade the *aruji* good-night; and his host showed him to a very small side-room, where a bed had been made ready. Then all went to sleep except the priest, who began to read the sûtras by the light of a paper lantern. Until a late hour he continued to read and pray: then he opened a little window in his little sleeping-room, to take a last look at the landscape before lying down. The night was beautiful: there was no cloud in the sky: there was no wind; and the strong moonlight threw down sharp black shadows of foliage, and glittered on the dews of the garden. Shrillings of crickets and bell-insects made a musical tumult; and the sound of the neighboring cascade deepened with the night. Kwairyō felt thirsty as he listened to the noise of the water; and, remembering the bamboo aqueduct at the rear of the house, he thought that he could go there and get a drink without disturbing the sleeping household. Very gently he pushed apart the sliding-screens that separated his room from the main apartment; and he saw, by the light of the lantern, five recumbent bodies—without heads!

For one instant he stood bewildered,—imagining a crime. But in another moment he perceived that there was no blood, and that the headless necks did not look as if they had been cut. Then he thought to himself:—"Either this is an illusion made by goblins, or I have been lured into the dwelling of a Rokuro-Kubi. ...In the book *Sōshinki* it is written that if one find the body of a Rokuro-Kubi without its head, and remove the body to another place, the head will never be able to join itself again to the neck. And the book further says that when the head comes back and finds that its body has been moved, it will strike itself upon the floor three times,—bounding like a ball,—and will pant as in great fear, and presently die. Now, if these be Rokuro-Kubi, they mean me no good;—so I shall be justified in following the instructions of the book.". . .

He seized the body of the *aruji* by the feet, pulled it to the window, and pushed it out. Then he went to the back-door, which he found barred; and he surmised that the heads had made their exit through the smoke-hole in the roof, which had been left open. Gently unbarring the door, he made his way to the garden, and proceeded with all possible caution to the grove beyond it. He heard voices talking in the grove; and he went in the direction of the voices,—stealing from shadow to shadow, until he reached a good hiding-place. Then, from behind a trunk, he caught sight of the heads,—all five of them,—flitting about, and chatting as they flitted. They were eating worms and insects which they found on the ground or among the trees. Presently the head of the *aruji* stopped eating and said:—

"Ah, that traveling priest who came to-night!—how fat all his body is! When we shall have eaten him, our bellies will be well filled. ...I was fool-ish to talk to him as I did;—it only set him to reciting the sûtras on behalf of my soul! To go near him while he is reciting would be difficult; and we cannot touch him so long as he is praying. But as it is now nearly morning, perhaps he has gone to sleep. ...Some one of you go to the house and see what the fellow is doing."

Another head—the head of a young woman—immediately rose up and flitted to the house, lightly as a bat. After a few minutes it came back, and cried out huskily, in a tone of great alarm:—

"That traveling priest is not in the house;—he is gone! But that is not the worst of the matter. He has taken the body of our *aruji*; and I do not know where he has put it."

At this announcement the head of the *aruji*—distinctly visible in the moonlight—assumed a frightful aspect: its eyes opened monstrously; its hair stood up bristling; and its teeth gnashed. Then a cry burst from its lips; and—weeping tears of rage—it exclaimed:—

"Since my body has been moved, to rejoin it is not possible! Then I must die! ... And all through the work of that priest! Before I die I will get at that priest!—I will tear him!—I will devour him!...And there he is— behind that tree!—hiding behind that tree! See him!—the fat coward!"...

In the same moment the head of the *aruji*, followed by the other four heads, sprang at Kwairyō. But the strong priest had already armed himself by plucking up a young tree; and with that tree he struck the heads as they came,—knocking them from him with tremendous blows. Four of them fled away. But the head of the *aruji*, though battered again and again, desperately continued to bound at the priest, and at last caught him by the left sleeve of his robe. Kwairyō, however, as quickly gripped the head by its topknot, and repeatedly struck it. It did not release its hold; but it uttered a long moan, and thereafter ceased to struggle. It was dead. But its teeth still held the sleeve; and, for all his great strength, Kwairyō could not force open the jaws.

With the head still hanging to his sleeve he went back to the house, and there caught sight of the other four Rokuro-Kubi squatting together, with their bruised and bleeding heads reunited to their bodies. But when they perceived him at the back-door all screamed, "The priest! the priest!"—and fled, through the other doorway, out into the woods.

Eastward the sky was brightening; day was about to dawn; and Kwairyō knew that the power of the goblins was limited to the hours of darkness. He looked at the head clinging to his sleeve,—its face all fouled with blood and foam and clay; and he laughed aloud as he thought to himself: "What a *miyagé*!⁴—the head of a goblin!" After which he gathered together his few belongings, and leisurely descended the mountain to continue his journey.

Right on he journeyed, until he came to Suwa in Shinano; and into the main street of Suwa he solemnly strode, with the head dangling at his elbow. Then woman fainted, and children screamed and ran away; and there was a great crowding and clamoring until the *torité* (as the police in those days were called) seized the priest, and took him to jail. For they sup-

---

4.   A present made to friends or to the household on returning from a journey is thus called. Ordinarily, of course, the *miyagé* consists of something produced in the locality to which the journey has been made: this is the point of Kwairyō's jest.

ROKURO-KUBI

||| 115 |||

posed the head to be the head of a murdered man who, in the moment of being killed, had caught the murderer's sleeve in his teeth. As for Kwairyō, he only smiled and said nothing when they questioned him. So, after having passed a night in prison, he was brought before the magistrates of the district. Then he was ordered to explain how he, a priest, had been found with the head of a man fastened to his sleeve, and why he had dared thus shamelessly to parade his crime in the sight of people.

Kwairyō laughed long and loudly at these questions; and then he said:—

"Sirs, I did not fasten the head to my sleeve: it fastened itself there— much against my will. And I have not committed any crime. For this is not the head of a man; it is the head of a goblin;—and, if I caused the death of the goblin, I did not do so by any shedding of blood, but simply by taking the precautions necessary to assure my own safety.". . . And he proceeded to relate the whole of the adventure,—bursting into another hearty laugh as he told of his encounter with the five heads.

But the magistrates did not laugh. They judged him to be a hardened criminal, and his story an insult to their intelligence. Therefore, without further questioning, they decided to order his immediate execution,—all of them except one, a very old man. This aged officer had made no remark during the trial; but, after having heard the opinion of his colleagues, he rose up, and said:—

"Let us first examine the head carefully; for this, I think, has not yet been done. If the priest has spoken truth, the head itself should bear witness for him . . . Bring the head here!"

So the head, still holding in its teeth the *koromo* that had been stripped from Kwairyō's shoulders, was put before the judges. The old man turned it round and round, carefully examined it, and discovered, on the nape of its neck, several strange red characters. He called the attention of his colleagues to these, and also bade them observe that the edges of the neck nowhere presented the appearance of having been cut by any weapon. On the contrary, the line of leverance was smooth as the line at which a falling leaf detaches itself from the stem ... Then said the elder:—

"I am quite sure that the priest told us nothing but the truth. This is the head of a Rokuro-Kubi. In the book *Nan-hō-ĭ-butsu-shi* it is written that certain red characters can always be found upon the nape of the neck of a real Rokuro-Kubi. There are the characters: you can see for yourselves that they have not been painted. Moreover, it is well known that such goblins have been dwelling in the mountains of the province of Kai from very ancient time. ... But you, Sir," he exclaimed, turning to Kwairyō,—"what sort of sturdy priest may you be? Certainly you have given proof of a courage that few priests possess; and you have the air of a soldier rather than a priest. Perhaps you once belonged to the samurai-class?"

"You have guessed rightly, Sir," Kwairyō responded. "Before becoming a priest, I long followed the profession of arms; and in those days I never feared man or devil. My name then was Isogai Héïdazaëmon Takétsura of Kyūshū: there may be some among you who remember it."

At the utterance of that name, a murmur of admiration filled the courtroom; for there were many present who remembered it. And Kwairyō immediately found himself among friends instead of judges,—friends anxious to prove their admiration by fraternal kindness. With honor they escorted him to the residence of the daimyō, who welcomed him, and feasted him, and made him a handsome present before allowing him to depart. When Kwairyō left Suwa, he was as happy as any priest is permitted to be in this transitory world. As for the head, he took it with him,—jocosely insisting that he intended it for a *miyagé*.

AND NOW it only remains to tell what became of the head.

A DAY OR TWO after leaving Suwa, Kwairyō met with a robber, who stopped him in a lonesome place, and bade him strip. Kwairyo at once removed his *koromo*, and offered it to the robber, who then first perceived what was hanging to the sleeve. Though brave, the highwayman was startled: he dropped the garment, and sprang back. Then he cried out:—"You!—what kind of a priest are you? Why, you are a worse man than I am! It is true that I have killed people; but I never walked about with anybody's head fastened to my sleeve.... Well, Sir priest, I suppose we are of the same calling; and I must say that I admire you!... Now that head would be of use to me: I could frighten people with it. Will you sell it? You can have my robe in exchange for your *koromo*; and I will give you five ryō for the head."

Kwairyō answered:—

"I shall let you have the head and the robe if you insist; but I must tell you that this is not the head of a man. It is a goblin's head. So, if you buy it, and have any trouble in consequence, please to remember that you were not deceived by me."

"What a nice priest you are!" exclaimed the robber. "You kill men, and jest about it!... But I am really in earnest. Here is my robe; and here is the money;—and let me have the head.... What is the use of joking?"

"Take the thing," said Kwairyo. "I was not joking. The only joke—if there be any joke at all—is that you are fool enough to pay good money for a goblin's head." And Kwairyō, loudly laughing, went upon his way.

THUS THE ROBBER got the head and the *koromo*; and for some time he played goblin-priest upon the highways. But, reaching the neighborhood of Suwa, he there leaned the true story of the head; and he then became afraid that the spirit of the Rokuro-Kubi might give him trouble. So he made up his mind to take back the head to the place from which it had come, and to bury it with its body. He found his way to the lonely cottage in the mountains of Kai; but nobody was there, and he could not discover the body. Therefore he buried the head by itself, in the grove behind the cottage; and he had a tombstone set up over the grave; and he caused a *Ségaki*-service to be performed on behalf of the spirit of the Rokuro-Kubi. And that tombstone—known as the Tombstone of the Rokuro-Kubi—may be seen (at least so the Japanese story-teller declares) even unto this day.

JUSTICE

THE TONGUE-CUT
SPARROW

Long, long ago in Japan there lived an old man and his wife. The old man was a good, kind-hearted, hard-working old fellow, but his wife was a regular cross-patch, who spoiled the happiness of her home by her scolding tongue. She was always grumbling about something from morning to night. The old man had for a long time ceased to take any notice of her crossness. He was out most of the day at work in the fields, and as he had no child, for his amusement when he came home, he kept a tame sparrow. He loved the little bird just as much as if she had been his child.

When he came back at night after his hard day's work in the open air it was his only pleasure to pet the sparrow, to talk to her and to teach her little tricks, which she learned very quickly. The old man would open her cage and let her fly about the room, and they would play together. Then when supper-time came, he always saved some tit-bits from his meal with which to feed his little bird.

Now one day the old man went out to chop wood in the forest, and the old woman stopped at home to wash clothes. The day before, she had made some starch, and now when she came to look for it, it was all gone; the bowl which she had filled full yesterday was quite empty.

While she was wondering who could have used or stolen the starch, down flew the pet sparrow, and bowing her little feathered head—a trick which she had been taught by her master—the pretty bird chirped and said:

"It is I who have taken the starch. I thought it was some food put out for me in that basin, and I ate it all. If I have made a mistake I beg you to forgive me! tweet, tweet, tweet!"

You see from this that the sparrow was a truthful bird, and the old woman ought to have been willing to forgive her at once when she asked her pardon so nicely. But not so.

The old woman had never loved the sparrow, and had often quarreled with her husband for keeping what she called a dirty bird about the house, saying that it only made extra work for her. Now she was only too delighted to have some cause of complaint against the pet. She scolded and even cursed the poor little bird for her bad behavior, and not content with using these harsh, unfeeling words, in a fit of rage she seized the sparrow—who all this time had spread out her wings and bowed her head before the old woman, to show how sorry she was—and fetched the scissors and cut off the poor little bird's tongue.

"I suppose you took my starch with that tongue! Now you may see what it is like to go without it!" And with these dreadful words she drove the bird away, not caring in the least what might happen to it and without the smallest pity for its suffering, so unkind was she!

The old woman, after she had driven the sparrow away, made some more rice-paste, grumbling all the time at the trouble, and after starching all her clothes, spread the things on boards to dry in the sun, instead of ironing them as they do in England.

In the evening the old man came home. As usual, on the way back he looked forward to the time when he should reach his gate and see his pet come flying and chirping to meet him, ruffling out her feathers to show her joy, and at last coming to rest on his shoulder. But to-night the old man was very disappointed, for not even the shadow of his dear sparrow was to be seen.

He quickened his steps, hastily drew off his straw sandals, and stepped on to the veranda. Still no sparrow was to be seen. He now felt sure that his wife, in one of her cross tempers, had shut the sparrow up in its cage. So he called her and said anxiously:

"Where is Suzume San (Miss Sparrow) today?"

The old woman pretended not to know at first, and answered:

"Your sparrow? I am sure I don't know. Now I come to think of it, I haven't seen her all the afternoon. I shouldn't wonder if the ungrateful bird had flown away and left you after all your petting!"

But at last, when the old man gave her no peace, but asked her again and again, insisting that she must know what had happened to his pet, she confessed all. She told him crossly how the sparrow had eaten the rice-paste she had specially made for starching her clothes, and how when the sparrow had confessed to what she had done, in great anger she had taken her scissors and cut out her tongue, and how finally she had driven the bird away and forbidden her to return to the house again.

Then the old woman showed her husband the sparrow's tongue, saying:

"Here is the tongue I cut off! Horrid little bird, why did it eat all my starch?"

"How could you be so cruel? Oh! how could you be so cruel?" was all that the old man could answer. He was too kind-hearted to punish his be shrew of a wife, but he was terribly distressed at what had happened to his poor little sparrow.

"What a dreadful misfortune for my poor Suzume San to lose her tongue!" he said to himself. "She won't be able to chirp any more, and surely the pain of the cutting of it out in that rough way must have made her ill! Is there nothing to be done?"

The old man shed many tears after his cross wife had gone to sleep. While he wiped away the tears with the sleeve of his cotton robe, a bright thought comforted him: he would go and look for the sparrow on the morrow. Having decided this he was able to go to sleep at last.

The next morning he rose early, as soon as ever the day broke, and snatching a hasty breakfast, started out over the hills and through the woods, stopping at every clump of bamboos to cry:

"Where, oh where does my tongue-cut sparrow stay? Where, oh where, does my tongue-cut sparrow stay!"

He never stopped to rest for his noonday meal, and it was far on in the afternoon when he found himself near a large bamboo wood. Bamboo groves are the favorite haunts of sparrows, and there sure enough at the edge of the wood he saw his own dear sparrow waiting to welcome him. He could hardly believe his eyes for joy, and ran forward quickly to greet her. She bowed her little head and went through a number of the tricks her master had taught her, to show her pleasure at seeing her old friend again, and, wonderful to relate, she could talk as of old. The old man told her how sorry he was for all that had happened, and inquired after her tongue, wondering how she could speak so well without it. Then the sparrow opened her beak and showed him that a new tongue had grown in place of the old one, and begged him not to think any more about the past, for she was quite well now. Then the old man knew that his sparrow was a fairy, and no common bird. It would be difficult to exaggerate the old man's rejoicing now. He forgot all his troubles, he forgot even how tired he was, for he had found his lost sparrow, and instead of being ill and without a tongue as he had feared and expected to find her, she was well and happy and with a new tongue, and without a sign of the ill-treatment she had received from his wife. And above all she was a fairy.

The sparrow asked him to follow her, and flying before him she led him to a beautiful house in the heart of the bamboo grove. The old man was utterly astonished when he entered the house to find what a beautiful place it was. It was built of the whitest wood, the soft cream-colored mats which took the place of carpets were the finest he had ever seen, and the cushions that the sparrow brought out for him to sit on were made of the finest silk and crape. Beautiful vases and lacquer boxes adorned the *tokonoma*[1] of every room.

---

1.   An alcove where precious objects are displayed.

The sparrow led the old man to the place of honor, and then, taking her place at a humble distance, she thanked him with many polite bows for all the kindness he had shown her for many long years.

Then the Lady Sparrow, as we will now call her, introduced all her family to the old man. This done, her daughters, robed in dainty crape gowns, brought in on beautiful old-fashioned trays a feast of all kinds of delicious foods, till the old man began to think he must be dreaming. In the middle of the dinner some of the sparrow's daughters performed a wonderful dance, called the "*Suzume-odori*" or the "Sparrow's dance," to amuse the guest.

Never had the old man enjoyed himself so much. The hours flew by too quickly in this lovely spot, with all these fairy sparrows to wait upon him and to feast him and to dance before him.

But the night came on and the darkness reminded him that he had a long way to go and must think about taking his leave and return home. He thanked his kind hostess for her splendid entertainment, and begged her for his sake to forget all she had suffered at the hands of his cross old wife. He told the Lady Sparrow that it was a great comfort and happiness to him to find her in such a beautiful home and to know that she wanted for nothing. It was his anxiety to know how she fared and what had really happened to her that had led him to seek her. Now he knew that all was well he could return home with a light heart. If ever she wanted him for anything she had only to send for him and he would come at once.

The Lady Sparrow begged him to stay and rest several days and enjoy the change, but the old man said he must return to his old wife—who would probably be cross at his not coming home at the usual time—and to his work, and therefore, much as he wished to do so, he could not accept her kind invitation. But now that he knew where the Lady Sparrow lived he would come to see her whenever he had the time.

When the Lady Sparrow saw that she could not persuade the old man to stay longer, she gave an order to some of her servants, and they at once brought in two boxes, one large and the other small. These were placed before the old man, and the Lady Sparrow asked him to choose whichever he liked for a present, which she wished to give him.

The old man could not refuse this kind proposal, and he chose the smaller box, saying:

"I am now too old and feeble to carry the big and heavy box. As you are so kind as to say that I may take whichever I like, I will choose the small one, which will be easier for me to carry."

Then the sparrows all helped him put it on his back and went to the gate to see him off, bidding him good-by with many bows and entreating him to come again whenever he had the time. Thus the old man and his pet sparrow separated quite happily, the sparrow showing not the least ill-will for all the unkindness she had suffered at the hands of the old wife. Indeed, she only felt sorrow for the old man who had to put up with it all his life.

When the old man reached home he found his wife even crosser than usual, for it was late on in the night and she had been waiting up for him for a long time.

"Where have you been all this time?" she asked in a big voice. "Why do you come back so late?"

The old man tried to pacify her by showing her the box of presents he had brought back with him, and then he told her of all that had happened to him, and how wonderfully he had been entertained at the sparrow's house.

"Now let us see what is in the box," said the old man, not giving her time to grumble again. "You must help me open it." And they both sat down before the box and opened it.

To their utter astonishment they found the box filled to the brim with gold and silver coins and many other precious things. The mats of their little cottage fairly glittered as they took out the things one by one and put them down and handled them over and over again. The old man was overjoyed at the sight of the riches that were now his. Beyond his brightest expectations was the sparrow's gift, which would enable him to give up work and live in ease and comfort the rest of his days.

He said: "Thanks to my good little sparrow! Thanks to my good little sparrow!" many times.

But the old woman, after the first moments of surprise and satisfaction at the sight of the gold and silver were over, could not suppress the greed of her wicked nature. She now began to reproach the old man for not having brought home the big box of presents, for in the innocence of his heart he had told her how he had refused the large box of presents which the sparrows had offered him, preferring the smaller one because it was light and easy to carry home.

"You silly old man." said she, "Why did you not bring the large box? Just think what we have lost. We might have had twice as much silver and gold as this. You are certainly an old fool!" she screamed, and then went to bed as angry as she could be.

The old man now wished that he had said nothing about the big box, but it was too late; the greedy old woman, not contented with the good luck which had so unexpectedly befallen them and which she so little deserved, made up her mind, if possible, to get more.

Early the next morning she got up and made the old man describe the way to the sparrow's house. When he saw what was in her mind he tried to keep her from going, but it was useless. She would not listen to one word he said. It is strange that the old woman did not feel ashamed of going to see the sparrow after the cruel way she had treated her in cutting off her tongue in a fit of rage. But her greed to get the big box made her forget everything else. It did not even enter her thoughts that the sparrows might be angry with her—as, indeed, they were—and might punish her for what she had done.

Ever since the Lady Sparrow had returned home in the sad plight in which they had first found her, weeping and bleeding from the mouth, her whole family and relations had done little else but speak of the cruelty of the old woman. "How could she," they asked each other, "inflict such a heavy punishment for such a trifling offense as that of eating some rice-paste by mistake?" They all loved the old man who was so kind and good and patient under all his troubles, but the old woman they hated, and they determined, if ever they had the chance, to punish her as she deserved. They had not long to wait.

After walking for some hours the old woman had at last found the bamboo grove which she had made her husband carefully describe, and now she stood before it crying out:

"Where is the tongue-cut sparrow's house? Where is the tongue-cut sparrow's house?"

At last she saw the eaves of the house peeping out from amongst the bamboo foliage. She hastened to the door and knocked loudly.

When the servants told the Lady Sparrow that her old mistress was at the door asking to see her, she was somewhat surprised at the unexpected visit, after all that had taken place, and she wondered not a little at the boldness of the old woman in venturing to come to the house. The Lady Sparrow, however, was a polite bird, and so she went out to greet the old woman, remembering that she had once been her mistress.

The old woman intended, however, to waste no time in words, she went right to the point, without the least shame, and said:

"You need not trouble to entertain me as you did my old man. I have come myself to get the box which he so stupidly left behind. I shall soon take my leave if you will give me the big box—that is all I want!"

The Lady Sparrow at once consented, and told her servants to bring out the big box. The old woman eagerly seized it and hoisted it on her back, and without even stopping to thank the Lady Sparrow began to hurry homewards.

The box was so heavy that she could not walk fast, much less run, as she would have liked to do, so anxious was she to get home and see what was inside the box, but she had often to sit down and rest herself by the way.

While she was staggering along under the heavy load, her desire to open the box became too great to be resisted. She could wait no longer, for she supposed this big box to be full of gold and silver and precious jewels like the small one her husband had received.

At last this greedy and selfish old woman put down the box by the wayside and opened it carefully, expecting to gloat her eyes on a mine of wealth. What she saw, however, so terrified her that she nearly lost her senses. As soon as she lifted the lid, a number of horrible and frightful looking demons bounced out of the box and surrounded her as if they intended to kill her. Not even in nightmares had she ever seen such horrible creatures as her much-coveted box contained. A demon with one huge eye right in the middle of its forehead came and glared at her, monsters with gaping mouths looked as if they would devour her, a huge snake coiled and hissed about her, and a big frog hopped and croaked towards her.

The old woman had never been so frightened in her life, and ran from the spot as fast as her quaking legs would carry her, glad to escape alive. When she reached home she fell to the floor and told her husband with tears all that had happened to her, and how she had been nearly killed by the demons in the box.

Then she began to blame the sparrow, but the old man stopped her at once, saying:

"Don't blame the sparrow, it is your wickedness which has at last met with its reward. I only hope this may be a lesson to you in the future!"

The old woman said nothing more, and from that day she repented of her cross, unkind ways, and by degrees became a good old woman, so that her husband hardly knew her to be the same person, and they spent their last days together happily, free from want or care, spending carefully the treasure the old man had received from his pet, the tongue-cut sparrow.

THE FARMER
and the BADGER

L ong, long ago, there lived an old farmer and his wife who had made their home in the mountains, far from any town. Their only neighbor was a bad and malicious badger. This badger used to come out every night and run across to the farmer's field and spoil the vegetables and the rice which the farmer spent his time in carefully cultivating. The badger at last grew so ruthless in his mischievous work, and did so much harm everywhere on the farm, that the good-natured farmer could not stand it any longer, and determined to put a stop to it. So he lay in wait day after day and night after night, with a big club, hoping to catch the badger, but all in vain. Then he laid traps for the wicked animal.

The farmer's trouble and patience was rewarded, for one fine day on going his rounds he found the badger caught in a hole he had dug for that purpose. The farmer was delighted at having caught his enemy, and carried him home securely bound with rope. When he reached the house the farmer said to his wife:

"I have at last caught the bad badger. You must keep an eye on him while I am out at work and not let him escape, because I want to make him into soup to-night."

Saying this, he hung the badger up to the rafters of his storehouse and went out to his work in the fields. The badger was in great distress, for he did not at all like the idea of being made into soup that night, and he thought and thought for a long time, trying to hit upon some plan by which he might escape. It was hard to think clearly in his uncomfortable position, for he had been hung upside down. Very near him, at the entrance to the storehouse, looking out towards the green fields and the trees and the pleasant sunshine, stood the farmer's old wife pounding barley. She looked tired and old. Her face was seamed with many wrinkles, and was as brown as leather, and every now and then she stopped to wipe the perspiration which rolled down her face.

"Dear lady," said the wily badger, "you must be very weary doing such heavy work in your old age. Won't you let me do that for you? My arms are very strong, and I could relieve you for a little while!"

"Thank you for your kindness," said the old woman, "but I cannot let you do this work for me because I must not untie you, for you might escape if I did, and my husband would be very angry if he came home and found you gone."

Now, the badger is one of the most cunning of animals, and he said again in a very sad, gentle, voice:

"You are very unkind. You might untie me, for I promise not to try to escape. If you are afraid of your husband, I will let you bind me again before his return when I have finished pounding the barley. I am so tired and sore tied up like this. If you would only let me down for a few minutes I would indeed be thankful!"

The old woman had a good and simple nature, and could not think badly of any one. Much less did she think that the badger was only deceiving her in order to get away. She felt sorry, too, for the animal as she turned to look at him. He looked in such a sad plight hanging downwards from the ceiling by his legs, which were all tied together so tightly that the rope and the knots were cutting into the skin. So in the kindness of her heart, and believing the creature's promise that he would not run away, she untied the cord and let him down.

The old woman then gave him the wooden pestle and told him to do the work for a short time while she rested. He took the pestle, but instead of doing the work as he was told, the badger at once sprang upon the old woman and knocked her down with the heavy piece of wood. He then killed her and cut her up and made soup of her, and waited for the return of the old farmer. The old man worked hard in his fields all day, and as he worked he thought with pleasure that no more now would his labor be spoiled by the destructive badger.

Towards sunset he left his work and turned to go home. He was very tired, but the thought of the nice supper of hot badger soup awaiting his return cheered him. The thought that the badger might get free and take revenge on the poor old woman never once came into his mind.

The badger meanwhile assumed the old woman's form, and as soon as he saw the old farmer approaching came out to greet him on the veranda of the little house, saying:

"So you have come back at last. I have made the badger soup and have been waiting for you for a long time."

The old farmer quickly took off his straw sandals and sat down before his tiny dinner-tray. The innocent man never even dreamed that it was not his wife but the badger who was waiting upon him, and asked at once for the soup. Then the badger suddenly transformed himself back to his natural form and cried out:

"You wife-eating old man! Look out for the bones in the kitchen!"

Laughing loudly and derisively he escaped out of the house and ran away to his den in the hills. The old man was left behind alone. He could hardly believe what he had seen and heard. Then when he understood the whole truth he was so scared and horrified that he fainted right away. After a while he came round and burst into tears. He cried loudly and bitterly. He rocked himself to and fro in his hopeless grief. It seemed too terrible to be real that his faithful old wife had been killed and cooked by the badger while he was working quietly in the fields, knowing nothing of what was going on at home, and congratulating himself on having once for all got rid of the wicked animal who had so often spoiled his fields. And oh! the horrible thought; he had very nearly drunk the soup which the creature had made of his poor old woman. "Oh dear, oh dear, oh dear!" he wailed aloud. Now, not far away there lived in the same mountain a kind, good-natured old rabbit. He heard the old man crying and sobbing and at once set out to see what was the matter, and if there was anything he could do to help his neighbor. The old man told him all that had happened. When the rabbit heard the story he was very angry at the wicked and deceitful badger, and told the old man to leave everything to him and he would avenge his wife's death. The farmer was at last comforted, and, wiping away his tears, thanked the rabbit for his goodness in coming to him in his distress.

The rabbit, seeing that the farmer was growing calmer, went back to his home to lay his plans for the punishment of the badger.

The next day the weather was fine, and the rabbit went out to find the badger. He was not to be seen in the woods or on the hillside or in the fields anywhere, so the rabbit went to his den and found the badger hiding there, for the animal had been afraid to show himself ever since he had escaped from the farmer's house, for fear of the old man's wrath.

The rabbit called out:

"Why are you not out on such a beautiful day? Come out with me, and we will go and cut grass on the hills together."

The badger, never doubting but that the rabbit was his friend, willingly consented to go out with him, only too glad to get away from the neighborhood of the farmer and the fear of meeting him. The rabbit led the way miles away from their homes, out on the hills where the grass grew tall and thick and sweet. They both set to work to cut down as much as they could carry home, to store it up for their winter's food. When they had each cut down all they wanted they tied it in bundles and then started homewards, each carrying his bundle of grass on his back. This time the rabbit made the badger go first.

When they had gone a little way the rabbit took out a flint and steel, and, striking it over the badger's back as he stepped along in front, set his bundle of grass on fire. The badger heard the flint striking, and asked:

"What is that noise. 'Crack, crack'?"

"Oh, that is nothing." replied the rabbit; "I only said 'Crack, crack' because this mountain is called Crackling Mountain."

The fire soon spread in the bundle of dry grass on the badger's back. The badger, hearing the crackle of the burning grass, asked, "What is that?"

"Now we have come to the 'Burning Mountain,'" answered the rabbit.

By this time the bundle was nearly burned out and all the hair had been burned off the badger's back. He now knew what had happened by the smell of the smoke of the burning grass. Screaming with pain the badger ran as fast as he could to his hole. The rabbit followed and found him lying on his bed groaning with pain.

"What an unlucky fellow you are!" said the rabbit. "I can't imagine how this happened! I will bring you some medicine which will heal your back quickly!"

The rabbit went away glad and smiling to think that the punishment upon the badger had already begun. He hoped that the badger would die of his burns, for he felt that nothing could be too bad for the animal, who was guilty of murdering a poor helpless old woman who had trusted him. He went home and made an ointment by mixing some sauce and red pepper together.

He carried this to the badger, but before putting it on he told him that it would cause him great pain, but that he must bear it patiently, because it was a very wonderful medicine for burns and scalds and such wounds. The badger thanked him and begged him to apply it at once. But no language can describe the agony of the badger as soon as the red pepper had been pasted all over his sore back. He rolled over and over and howled loudly. The rabbit, looking on, felt that the farmer's wife was beginning to be avenged.

The badger was in bed for about a month; but at last, in spite of the red pepper application, his burns healed and he got well. When the rabbit saw that the badger was getting well, he thought of another plan by which he could compass the creature's death. So he went one day to pay the badger a visit and to congratulate him on his recovery.

During the conversation the rabbit mentioned that he was going fishing, and described how pleasant fishing was when the weather was fine and the sea smooth.

The badger listened with pleasure to the rabbit's account of the way he passed his time now, and forgot all his pains and his month's illness, and thought what fun it would be if he could go fishing too; so he asked the rabbit if he would take him the next time he went out to fish. This was just what the rabbit wanted, so he agreed.

Then he went home and built two boats, one of wood and the other of clay. At last they were both finished, and as the rabbit stood and looked at his work he felt that all his trouble would be well rewarded if his plan succeeded, and he could manage to kill the wicked badger now.

The day came when the rabbit had arranged to take the badger fishing. He kept the wooden boat himself and gave the badger the clay boat. The badger, who knew nothing about boats, was delighted with his new boat and thought how kind it was of the rabbit to give it to him. They both got into their boats and set out. After going some distance from the shore the rabbit proposed that they should try their boats and see which one could go the quickest. The badger fell in with the proposal, and they both set to work to row as fast as they could for some time. In the middle of the race the badger found his boat going to pieces, for the water now began to soften the clay. He cried out in great fear to the rabbit to help him. But the rabbit answered that he was avenging the old woman's murder, and that this had been his intention all along, and that he was happy to think that the badger had at last met his deserts for all his evil crimes, and was to drown with no one to help him. Then he raised his oar and struck at the badger with all his strength till he fell with the sinking clay boat and was seen no more.

Thus at last he kept his promise to the old farmer. The rabbit now turned and rowed shorewards, and having landed and pulled his boat upon the beach, hurried back to tell the old farmer everything, and how the badger, his enemy, had been killed.

The old farmer thanked him with tears in his eyes. He said that till now he could never sleep at night or be at peace in the daytime, thinking of how his wife's death was unavenged, but from this time he would be able to sleep and eat as of old. He begged the rabbit to stay with him and share his home, so from this day the rabbit went to stay with the old farmer and they both lived together as good friends to the end of their days.

THE STORY of the OLD MAN WHO MADE WITHERED TREES to FLOWER

Long, long ago there lived an old man and his wife who supported themselves by cultivating a small plot of land. Their life had been a very happy and peaceful one save for one great sorrow, and this was they had no child. Their only pet was a dog named Shiro, and on him they lavished all the affection of their old age. Indeed, they loved him so much that whenever they had anything nice to eat they denied themselves to give it to Shiro. Now Shiro means "white," and he was so called because of his color. He was a real Japanese dog, and very like a small wolf in appearance.

The happiest hour of the day both for the old man and his dog was when the man returned from his work in the field, and having finished his frugal supper of rice and vegetables, would take what he had saved from the meal out to the little veranda that ran round the cottage. Sure enough, Shiro was waiting for his master and the evening tit-bit. Then the old man said "Chin, chin!" and Shiro sat up and begged, and his master gave him the food. Next door to this good old couple there lived another old man and his wife who were both wicked and cruel, and who hated their good neighbors and the dog Shiro with all their might. Whenever Shiro happened to look into their kitchen they at once kicked him or threw something at him, sometimes even wounding him.

One day Shiro was heard barking for a long time in the field at the back of his master's house. The old man, thinking that perhaps some birds were attacking the corn, hurried out to see what was the matter. As soon as Shiro saw his master he ran to meet him, wagging his tail, and, seizing the end of his *kimono*, dragged him under a large yenoki tree. Here he began to dig very industriously with his paws, yelping with joy all the time. The old man, unable to understand what it all meant, stood looking on in bewilderment. But Shiro went on barking and digging with all his might.

The thought that something might be hidden beneath the tree, and that the dog had scented it, at last struck the old man. He ran back to the house, fetched his spade and began to dig the ground at that spot. What was his astonishment when, after digging for some time, he came upon a heap of old and valuable coins, and the deeper he dug the more gold coins did he find. So intent was the old man on his work that he never saw the cross face of his neighbor peering at him through the bamboo hedge. At last all the gold coins lay shining on the ground. Shiro sat by erect with pride and looking fondly at his master as if to say, "You see, though only a dog, I can make some return for all the kindness you show me."

The old man ran in to call his wife, and together they carried home the treasure. Thus in one day the poor old man became rich. His gratitude to the faithful dog knew no bounds, and he loved and petted him more than ever, if that were possible.

The cross old neighbor, attracted by Shiro's barking, had been an unseen and envious witness of the finding of the treasure. He began to think that he, too, would like to find a fortune. So a few days later he called at the old man's house and very ceremoniously asked permission to borrow Shiro for a short time.

Shiro's master thought this a strange request, because he knew quite well that not only did his neighbor not love his pet dog, but that he never lost an opportunity of striking and tormenting him whenever the dog crossed his path. But the good old man was too kind-hearted to refuse his neighbor, so he consented to lend the dog on condition that he should be taken great care of.

The wicked old man returned to his home with an evil smile on his face, and told his wife how he had succeeded in his crafty intentions. He then took his spade and hastened to his own field, forcing the unwilling Shiro to follow him. As soon as he reached a yenoki tree, he said to the dog, threateningly:

"If there were gold coins under your master's tree, there must also be gold coins under my tree. You must find them for me! Where are they? Where? Where?"

And catching hold of Shiro's neck he held the dog's head to the ground, so that Shiro began to scratch and dig in order to free himself from the horrid old man's grasp.

The old man was very pleased when he saw the dog begin to scratch and dig, for he at once supposed that some gold coins lay buried under his tree as well as under his neighbor's, and that the dog had scented them as before; so pushing Shiro away he began to dig himself, but there was nothing to be found. As he went on digging a foul smell was noticeable, and he at last came upon a refuse heap.

The old man's disgust can be imagined. This soon gave way to anger. He had seen his neighbor's good fortune, and hoping for the same luck himself, he had borrowed the dog Shiro; and now, just as he seemed on the point of finding what he sought, only a horrid smelling refuse heap had rewarded him for a morning's digging. Instead of blaming his own greed for his disappointment, he blamed the poor dog. He seized his spade, and with all his strength struck Shiro and killed him on the spot. He then threw the dog's body into the hole which he had dug in the hope of finding a treasure of gold coins, and covered it over with the earth. Then he returned to the house, telling no one, not even his wife, what he had done.

After waiting several days, as the dog Shiro did not return, his master began to grow anxious. Day after day went by and the good old man waited in vain. Then he went to his neighbor and asked him to give him back his dog. Without any shame or hesitation, the wicked neighbor answered that he had killed Shiro because of his bad behavior. At this dreadful news Shiro's master wept many sad and bitter tears. Great indeed, was his woeful surprise, but he was too good and gentle to reproach his bad neighbor. Learning that Shiro was buried under the yenoki tree in the field, he asked the old man to give him the tree, in remembrance of his poor dog Shiro.

Even the cross old neighbor could not refuse such a simple request, so he consented to give the old man the tree under which Shiro lay buried. Shiro's master then cut the tree down and carried it home. Out of the trunk he made a mortar. In this his wife put some rice, and he began to pound it with the intention of making a festival to the memory of his dog Shiro.

A strange thing happened! His wife put the rice into the mortar, and no sooner had he begun to pound it to make the cakes, than it began to increase in quantity gradually till it was about five times the original amount, and the cakes were turned out of the mortar as if an invisible hand were at work.

When the old man and his wife saw this, they understood that it was a reward to them from Shiro for their faithful love to him. They tasted the cakes and found them nicer than any other food. So from this time they never troubled about food, for they lived upon the cakes with which the mortar never ceased to supply them.

The greedy neighbor, hearing of this new piece of good luck, was filled with envy as before, and called on the old man and asked leave to borrow the wonderful mortar for a short time, pretending that he, too, sorrowed for the death of Shiro, and wished to make cakes for a festival to the dog's memory.

The old man did not in the least wish to lend it to his cruel neighbor, but he was too kind to refuse. So the envious man carried home the mortar, but he never brought it back.

Several days passed, and Shiro's master waited in vain for the mortar, so he went to call on the borrower, and asked him to be good enough to return the mortar if he had finished with it. He found him sitting by a big fire made of pieces of wood. On the ground lay what looked very much like pieces of a broken mortar. In answer to the old man's inquiry, the wicked neighbor answered haughtily:

"Have you come to ask me for your mortar? I broke it to pieces, and now I am making a fire of the wood, for when I tried to pound cakes in it only some horrid smelling stuff came out."

The good old man said:

"I am very sorry for that. It is a great pity you did not ask me for the cakes if you wanted them. I would have given you as many as ever you wanted. Now please give me the ashes of the mortar, as I wish to keep them in remembrance of my dog."

The neighbor consented at once, and the old man carried home a basket full of ashes.

Not long after this the old man accidentally scattered some of the ashes made by the burning of the mortar on the trees of his garden. A wonderful thing happened!

It was late in autumn and all the trees had shed their leaves, but no sooner did the ashes touch their branches than the cherry trees, the plum trees, and all other blossoming shrubs burst into bloom, so that the old man's garden was suddenly transformed into a beautiful picture of spring. The old man's delight knew no bounds, and he carefully preserved the remaining ashes.

The story of the old man's garden spread far and wide, and people from far and near came to see the wonderful sight.

One day, soon after this, the old man heard some one knocking at his door, and going to the porch to see who it was he was surprised to see a Knight standing there. This Knight told him that he was a retainer of a

THE STORY OF THE OLD MAN

‖ 145 ‖

great Daimio (Earl); that one of the favorite cherry trees in this nobleman's garden had withered, and that though every one in his service had tried all manner of means to revive it, none took effect. The Knight was sore perplexed when he saw what great displeasure the loss of his favorite cherry tree caused the Daimio. At this point, fortunately, they had heard that there was a wonderful old man who could make withered trees to blossom, and his Lord had sent him to ask the old man to come to him.

"And," added the Knight, "I shall be very much obliged if you will come at once."

The good old man was greatly surprised at what he heard, but respectfully followed the Knight to the nobleman's Palace.

The Daimio, who had been impatiently awaiting the old man's coming, as soon as he saw him asked him at once:

"Are you the old man who can make withered trees flower even out of season?"

The old man made an obeisance, and replied:

"I am that old man!"

Then the Daimio said:

"You must make that dead cherry tree in my garden blossom again by means of your famous ashes. I shall look on."

Then they all went into the garden—the Daimio and his retainers and the ladies-in-waiting, who carried the Daimio's sword.

The old man now tucked up his *kimono* and made ready to climb the tree. Saying "Excuse me," he took the pot of ashes which he had brought with him, and began to climb the tree, everyone watching his movements with great interest.

At last he climbed to the spot where the tree divided into two great branches, and taking up his position here, the old man sat down and scattered the ashes right and left all over the branches and twigs.

Wonderful, indeed, was the result! The withered tree at once burst into full bloom! The Daimio was so transported with joy that he looked as if he would go mad. He rose to his feet and spread out his fan, calling the old man down from the tree. He himself gave the old man a wine cup filled with the best *saké*, and rewarded him with much silver and gold and many other precious things. The Daimio ordered that henceforth the old man should call himself by the name of *Hana-Saka-Jijii*, or "The Old Man who makes the Trees to Blossom," and that henceforth all were to recognize him by this name, and he sent him home with great honor.

The wicked neighbor, as before, heard of the good old man's fortune, and of all that had so auspiciously befallen him, and he could not suppress all the envy and jealousy that filled his heart. He called to mind how he had failed in his attempt to find the gold coins, and then in making the magic cakes; this time surely he must succeed if he imitated the old man, who made withered trees to flower simply by sprinkling ashes on them. This would be the simplest task of all.

So he set to work and gathered together all the ashes which remained in the fire-place from the burning of the wonderful mortar. Then he set out in the hope of finding some great man to employ him, calling out loudly as he went along:

"Here comes the wonderful man who can make withered trees blossom! Here comes the old man who can make dead trees blossom!"

The Daimio in his Palace heard this cry, and said:

"That must be the *Hana-Saka-Jijii* passing. I have nothing to do to-day. Let him try his art again; it will amuse me to look on."

So the retainers went out and brought in the impostor before their Lord. The satisfaction of the false old man can now be imagined.

But the Daimio looking at him, thought it strange that he was not at all like the old man he had seen before, so he asked him:

"Are you the man whom I named *Hana-Saka-Jijii*?"

And the envious neighbor answered with a lie:

"Yes, my Lord!"

"That is strange!" said the Daimio. "I thought there was only one *Hana-Saka-Jijii* in the world! Has he now some disciples?"

"I am the true *Hana-Saka-Jijii*. The one who came to you before was only my disciple!" replied the old man again.

"Then you must be more skillful than the other. Try what you can do and let me see!"

The envious neighbor, with the Daimio and his Court following, then went into the garden, and approaching a dead tree, took out a handful of the ashes which he carried with him, and scattered them over the tree.

But not only did the tree not burst into flower, but not even a bud came forth. Thinking that he had not used enough ashes, the old man took handfuls and again sprinkled them over the withered tree. But all to no effect. After trying several times, the ashes were blown into the Daimio's eyes. This made him very angry, and he ordered his retainers to arrest the false *Hana-Saka-Jijii* at once and put him in prison for an impostor. From this imprisonment the wicked old man was never freed. Thus did he meet with punishment at last for all his evil doings.

The good old man, however, with the treasure of gold coins which Shiro had found for him, and with all the gold and the silver which the Daimio had showered on him, became a rich and prosperous man in his old age, and lived a long and happy life, beloved and respected by all.

THE MIRROR of MATSUYAMA:
A STORY of OLD JAPAN

L ong years ago in old Japan there lived in the Province of Echigo, a very remote part of Japan even in these days, a man and his wife. When this story begins they had been married for some years and were blessed with one little daughter. She was the joy and pride of both their lives, and in her they stored an endless source of happiness for their old age.

What golden letter days in their memory were these that had marked her growing up from babyhood; the visit to the temple when she was just thirty days old, her proud mother carrying her, robed in ceremonial *kimono*, to be put under the patronage of the family's household god; then her first dolls festival, when her parents gave her a set of dolls and their miniature belongings, to be added to as year succeeded year; and perhaps the most important occasion of all, on her third birthday, when her first *obi* (broad brocade sash) of scarlet and gold was tied round her small waist, a sign that she had crossed the threshold of girlhood and left infancy behind. Now that she was seven years of age, and had learned to talk and to wait upon her parents in those several little ways so dear to the hearts of fond parents, their cup of happiness seemed full. There could not be found in the whole of the Island Empire a happier little family.

One day there was much excitement in the home, for the father had been suddenly summoned to the capital on business. In these days of railways and jinrickshas and other rapid modes of traveling, it is difficult to realize what such a journey as that from Matsuyama to Kyoto meant. The roads were rough and bad, and ordinary people had to walk every step of the way, whether the distance were one hundred or several hundred miles. Indeed, in those days it was as great an undertaking to go up to the capital as it is for a Japanese to make a voyage to Europe now.

So the wife was very anxious while she helped her husband get ready for the long journey, knowing what an arduous task lay before him. Vainly she wished that she could accompany him, but the distance was too great for the mother and child to go, and besides that, it was the wife's duty to take care of the home.

All was ready at last, and the husband stood in the porch with his little family round him.

"Do not be anxious, I will come back soon," said the man. "While I am away take care of everything, and especially of our little daughter."

"Yes, we shall be all right—but you—you must take care of yourself and delay not a day in coming back to us," said the wife, while the tears fell like rain from her eyes.

The little girl was the only one to smile, for she was ignorant of the sorrow of parting, and did not know that going to the capital was at all different from walking to the next village, which her father did very often. She ran to his side, and caught hold of his long sleeve to keep him a moment.

"Father, I will be very good while I am waiting for you to come back, so please bring me a present."

As the father turned to take a last look at his weeping wife and smiling, eager child, he felt as if some one were pulling him back by the hair, so hard was it for him to leave them behind, for they had never been separated before. But he knew that he must go, for the call was imperative. With a great effort he ceased to think, and resolutely turning away he went quickly down the little garden and out through the gate. His wife, catching up the child in her arms, ran as far as the gate, and watched him as he went down the road between the pines till he was lost in the haze of the distance and all she could see was his quaint peaked hat, and at last that vanished too.

"Now father has gone, you and I must take care of everything till he comes back," said the mother, as she made her way back to the house.

"Yes, I will be very good," said the child, nodding her head, "and when father comes home please tell him how good I have been, and then perhaps he will give me a present."

"Father is sure to bring you something that you want very much. I know, for I asked him to bring you a doll. You must think of father every day, and pray for a safe journey till he comes back."

"O, yes, when he comes home again how happy I shall be," said the child, clapping her hands, and her face growing bright with joy at the glad thought. It seemed to the mother as she looked at the child's face that her love for her grew deeper and deeper.

Then she set to work to make the winter clothes for the three of them. She set up her simple wooden spinning-wheel and spun the thread before she began to weave the stuffs. In the intervals of her work she directed the little girl's games and taught her to read the old stories of her country. Thus did the wife find consolation in work during the lonely days of her husband's absence. While the time was thus slipping quickly by in the quiet home, the husband finished his business and returned.

It would have been difficult for any one who did not know the man well to recognize him. He had traveled day after day, exposed to all weathers, for about a month altogether, and was sunburnt to bronze, but his fond wife and child knew him at a glance, and flew to meet him from either side, each catching hold of one of his sleeves in their eager greeting. Both the man and his wife rejoiced to find each other well. It seemed a very long time to all till—the mother and child helping—his straw sandals were untied, his large umbrella hat taken off, and he was again in their midst in the old familiar sitting-room that had been so empty while he was away.

As soon as they had sat down on the white mats, the father opened a bamboo basket that he had brought in with him, and took out a beautiful doll and a lacquer box full of cakes.

"Here," he said to the little girl, "is a present for you. It is a prize for taking care of mother and the house so well while I was away."

"Thank you," said the child, as she bowed her head to the ground, and then put out her hand just like a little maple leaf with its eager wide-spread fingers to take the doll and the box, both of which, coming from the capital, were prettier than anything she had ever seen. No words can tell how delighted the little girl was—her face seemed as if it would melt with joy, and she had no eyes and no thought for anything else.

Again the husband dived into the basket, and brought out this time a square wooden box, carefully tied up with red and white string, and handing it to his wife, said:

"And this is for you."

The wife took the box, and opening it carefully took out a metal disk with a handle attached. One side was bright and shining like a crystal, and the other was covered with raised figures of pine-trees and storks, which had been carved out of its smooth surface in lifelike reality. Never had she seen such a thing in her life, for she had been born and bred in the rural province of Echigo. She gazed into the shining disk, and looking up with surprise and wonder pictured on her face, she said:

"I see somebody looking at me in this round thing! What is it that you have given me?"

The husband laughed and said:

"Why, it is your own face that you see. What I have brought you is called a mirror, and whoever looks into its clear surface can see their own form reflected there. Although there are none to be found in this out of the way place, yet they have been in use in the capital from the most ancient times.

There the mirror is considered a very necessary requisite for a woman to possess. There is an old proverb that 'As the sword is the soul of a samurai, so is the mirror the soul of a woman,' and according to popular tradition, a woman's mirror is an index to her own heart—if she keeps it bright and clear, so is her heart pure and good. It is also one of the treasures that form the insignia of the Emperor. So you must lay great store by your mirror, and use it carefully."

The wife listened to all her husband told her, and was pleased at learning so much that was new to her. She was still more pleased at the precious gift—his token of remembrance while he had been away.

"If the mirror represents my soul, I shall certainly treasure it as a valuable possession, and never will I use it carelessly." Saying so, she lifted it as high as her forehead, in grateful acknowledgment of the gift, and then shut it up in its box and put it away.

The wife saw that her husband was very tired, and set about serving the evening meal and making everything as comfortable as she could for him. It seemed to the little family as if they had not known what true happiness was before, so glad were they to be together again, and this evening the father had much to tell of his journey and of all he had seen at the great capital.

Time passed away in the peaceful home, and the parents saw their fondest hopes realized as their daughter grew from childhood into a beautiful girl of sixteen. As a gem of priceless value is held in its proud owner's hand, so had they reared her with unceasing love and care: and now their pains were more than doubly rewarded. What a comfort she was to her mother as she went about the house taking her part in the housekeeping, and how proud her father was of her, for she daily reminded him of her mother when he had first married her.

But, alas! in this world nothing lasts forever. Even the moon is not always perfect in shape, but loses its roundness with time, and flowers bloom and then fade. So at last the happiness of this family was broken up by a great sorrow. The good and gentle wife and mother was one day taken ill.

In the first days of her illness the father and daughter thought that it was only a cold, and were not particularly anxious. But the days went by and still the mother did not get better; she only grew worse, and the doctor was puzzled, for in spite of all he did the poor woman grew weaker day by day. The father and daughter were stricken with grief, and day or night the girl never left her mother's side. But in spite of all their efforts the woman's life was not to be saved.

One day as the girl sat near her mother's bed, trying to hide with a cheery smile the gnawing trouble at her heart, the mother roused herself and taking her daughter's hand, gazed earnestly and lovingly into her eyes. Her breath was labored and she spoke with difficulty:

"My daughter. I am sure that nothing can save me now. When I am dead, promise me to take care of your dear father and to try to be a good and dutiful woman."

"Oh, mother," said the girl as the tears rushed to her eyes, "you must not say such things. All you have to do is to make haste and get well—that will bring the greatest happiness to father and myself."

"Yes, I know, and it is a comfort to me in my last days to know how greatly you long for me to get better, but it is not to be. Do not look so sorrowful, for it was so ordained in my previous state of existence that I should die in this life just at this time; knowing this, I am quite resigned to my fate. And now I have something to give you whereby to remember me when I am gone."

Putting her hand out, she took from the side of the pillow a square wooden box tied up with a silken cord and tassels. Undoing this very carefully, she took out of the box the mirror that her husband had given her years ago.

"When you were still a little child your father went up to the capital and brought me back as a present this treasure; it is called a mirror. This I give you before I die. If, after I have ceased to be in this life, you are lonely and long to see me sometimes, then take out this mirror and in the clear and shining surface you will always see me—so will you be able to meet with me often and tell me all your heart; and though I shall not be able to speak, I shall understand and sympathize with you, whatever may happen to you in the future." With these words the dying woman handed the mirror to her daughter.

The mind of the good mother seemed to be now at rest, and sinking back without another word her spirit passed quietly away that day.

The bereaved father and daughter were wild with grief, and they abandoned themselves to their bitter sorrow. They felt it to be impossible to take leave of the loved woman who till now had filled their whole lives and to commit her body to the earth. But this frantic burst of grief passed, and then they took possession of their own hearts again, crushed though they were in resignation. In spite of this the daughter's life seemed to her desolate. Her love for her dead mother did not grow less with time, and so keen was her remembrance, that everything in daily life, even the falling of the rain and the blowing of the wind, reminded her of her mother's death and of all that they had loved and shared together. One day when her father was out, and she was fulfilling her household duties alone, her loneliness and sorrow seemed more than she could bear. She threw herself down in her mother's room and wept as if her heart would break. Poor child, she longed just for one glimpse of the loved face, one sound of the voice calling her pet name, or for one moment's forgetfulness of the aching void in her heart. Suddenly she sat up. Her mother's last words had rung through her memory hitherto dulled by grief.

"Oh! my mother told me when she gave me the mirror as a parting gift, that whenever I looked into it I should be able to meet her—to see her. I had nearly forgotten her last words—how stupid I am; I will get the mirror now and see if it can possibly be true!"

She dried her eyes quickly, and going to the cupboard took out the box that contained the mirror, her heart beating with expectation as she lifted the mirror out and gazed into its smooth face. Behold, her mother's words were true! In the round mirror before her she saw her mother's face; but, oh, the joyful surprise! It was not her mother thin and wasted by illness, but the young and beautiful woman as she remembered her far back in the days of her own earliest childhood. It seemed to the girl that the face in the mirror must soon speak, almost that she heard the voice of her mother telling her again to grow up a good woman and a dutiful daughter, so earnestly did the eyes in the mirror look back into her own.

"It is certainly my mother's soul that I see. She knows how miserable I am without her and she has come to comfort me. Whenever I long to see her she will meet me here; how grateful I ought to be!"

And from this time the weight of sorrow was greatly lightened for her young heart. Every morning, to gather strength for the day's duties before her, and every evening, for consolation before she lay down to rest, did the young girl take out the mirror and gaze at the reflection which in the simplicity of her innocent heart she believed to be her mother's soul. Daily she grew in the likeness of her dead mother's character, and was gentle and kind to all, and a dutiful daughter to her father.

A year spent in mourning had thus passed away in the little household, when, by the advice of his relations, the man married again, and the daughter now found herself under the authority of a step-mother. It was a trying position; but her days spent in the recollection of her own beloved mother, and of trying to be what that mother would wish her to be, had made the young girl docile and patient, and she now determined to be filial and dutiful to her father's wife, in all respects. Everything went on apparently smoothly in the family for some time under the new *régime*; there were no winds or waves of discord to ruffle the surface of every-day life, and the father was content.

But it is a woman's danger to be petty and mean, and step-mothers are proverbial all the world over, and this one's heart was not as her first smiles were. As the days and weeks grew into months, the step-mother began to treat the motherless girl unkindly and to try and come between the father and child.

Sometimes she went to her husband and complained of her step-daughter's behavior, but the father knowing that this was to be expected, took no notice of her ill-natured complaints. Instead of lessening his affection for his daughter, as the woman desired, her grumblings only made him think of her the more. The woman soon saw that he began to show more concern for his lonely child than before. This did not please her at all, and she began to turn over in her mind how she could, by some means or other, drive her step-child out of the house. So crooked did the woman's heart become.

She watched the girl carefully, and one day peeping into her room in the early morning, she thought she discovered a grave enough sin of which to accuse the child to her father. The woman herself was a little frightened too at what she had seen.

So she went at once to her husband, and wiping away some false tears she said in a sad voice:

"Please give me permission to leave you today."

The man was completely taken by surprise at the suddenness of her request, and wondered whatever was the matter.

"Do you find it so disagreeable," he asked, "in my house, that you can stay no longer?"

"No! no! it has nothing to do with you—even in my dreams I have never thought that I wished to leave your side; but if I go on living here I am in danger of losing my life, so I think it best for all concerned that you should allow me to go home!"

And the woman began to weep afresh. Her husband, distressed to see her so unhappy, and thinking that he could not have heard aright, said:

"Tell me what you mean! How is your life in danger here?"

"I will tell you since you ask me. Your daughter dislikes me as her step-mother. For some time past she has shut herself up in her room morning and evening, and looking in as I pass by, I am convinced that she has made an image of me and is trying to kill me by magic art, cursing me daily. It is not safe for me to stay here, such being the case; indeed, indeed, I must go away, we cannot live under the same roof any more."

The husband listened to the dreadful tale, but he could not believe his gentle daughter guilty of such an evil act. He knew that by popular super-stition people believed that one person could cause the gradual death of another by making an image of the hated one and cursing it daily; but where had his young daughter learned such knowledge?—the thing was impossible. Yet he remembered having noticed that his daughter stayed much in her room of late and kept herself away from every one, even when visitors came to the house. Putting this fact together with his wife's alarm, he thought that there might be something to account for the strange story.

His heart was torn between doubting his wife and trusting his child, and he knew not what to do. He decided to go at once to his daughter and try to find out the truth. Comforting his wife and assuring her that her fears were groundless, he glided quietly to his daughter's room.

The girl had for a long time past been very unhappy. She had tried by amiability and obedience to show her goodwill and to mollify the new wife, and to break down that wall of prejudice and misunderstanding that she knew generally stood between step-parents and their step-children. But she soon found that her efforts were in vain. The step-mother never trusted her, and seemed to misinterpret all her actions, and the poor child knew very well that she often carried unkind and untrue tales to her father. She could not help comparing her present unhappy condition with the time when her own mother was alive only a little more than a year ago—so great a change in this short time! Morning and evening she wept over the remembrance. Whenever she could she went to her room, and sliding the screens to, took out the mirror and gazed, as she thought, at her mother's face. It was the only comfort that she had in these wretched days.

Her father found her occupied in this way. Pushing aside the *fusama*, he saw her bending over something or other very intently. Looking over her shoulder, to see who was entering her room, the girl was surprised to see her father, for he generally sent for her when he wished to speak to her. She was also confused at being found looking at the mirror, for she had never told any one of her mother's last promise, but had kept it as the sacred secret of her heart. So before turning to her father she slipped the mirror into her long sleeve. Her father noting her confusion, and her act of hiding something, said in a severe manner:

"Daughter, what are you doing here? And what is that that you have hidden in your sleeve?"

The girl was frightened by her father's severity. Never had he spoken to her in such a tone. Her confusion changed to apprehension, her color from scarlet to white. She sat dumb and shamefaced, unable to reply.

Appearances were certainly against her; the young girl looked guilty, and the father thinking that perhaps after all what his wife had told him was true, spoke angrily:

"Then, is it really true that you are daily cursing your step-mother and praying for her death? Have you forgotten what I told you, that although she is your step-mother you must be obedient and loyal to her? What evil spirit has taken possession of your heart that you should be so wicked? You have certainly changed, my daughter! What has made you so disobedient and unfaithful?"

And the father's eyes filled with sudden tears to think that he should have to upbraid his daughter in this way.

She on her part did not know what he meant, for she had never heard of the superstition that by praying over an image it is possible to cause the death of a hated person. But she saw that she must speak and clear herself somehow. She loved her father dearly, and could not bear the idea of his anger. She put out her hand on his knee deprecatingly:

"Father! father! do not say such dreadful things to me. I am still your obedient child. Indeed, I am. However stupid I may be, I should never be able to curse any one who belonged to you, much less pray for the death of one you love. Surely some one has been telling you lies, and you are dazed, and you know not what you say—or some evil spirit has taken possession of *your* heart. As for me I do not know—no, not so much as a dew-drop, of the evil thing of which you accuse me."

But the father remembered that she had hidden something away when he first entered the room, and even this earnest protest did not satisfy him. He wished to clear up his doubts once for all.

"Then why are you always alone in your room these days? And tell me what is that that you have hidden in your sleeve—show it to me at once."

Then the daughter, though shy of confessing how she had cherished her mother's memory, saw that she must tell her father all in order to clear herself. So she slipped the mirror out from her long sleeve and laid it before him.

"This," she said, "is what you saw me looking at just now."

"Why," he said in great surprise, "this is the mirror that I brought as a gift to your mother when I went up to the capital many years ago! And so you have kept it all this time? Now, why do you spend so much of your time before this mirror?"

Then she told him of her mother's last words, and of how she had promised to meet her child whenever she looked into the glass. But still the father could not understand the simplicity of his daughter's character in not knowing that what she saw reflected in the mirror was in reality her own face, and not that of her mother.

"What do you mean?" he asked. "I do not understand how you can meet the soul of your lost mother by looking in this mirror."

"It is indeed true," said the girl: "and if you don't believe what I say, look for yourself," and she placed the mirror before her. There, looking back from the smooth metal disk, was her own sweet face. She pointed to the reflection seriously:

"Do you doubt me still?" she asked earnestly, looking up into his face.

With an exclamation of sudden understanding the father smote his two hands together.

"How stupid I am! At last I understand. Your face is as like your mother's as the two sides of a melon—thus you have looked at the reflection of your face all this time, thinking that you were brought face to face with your lost mother! You are truly a faithful child. It seems at first a stupid thing to have done, but it is not really so. It shows how deep has been your filial piety, and how innocent your heart. Living in constant remembrance of your lost mother has helped you to grow like her in character. How clever it was of her to tell you to do this. I admire and respect you, my daughter, and I am ashamed to think that for one instant I believed your suspicious step-mother's story and suspected you of evil, and came with the intention of scolding you severely, while all this time you have been so true and good. Before you I have no countenance left, and I beg you to forgive me."

And here the father wept. He thought of how lonely the poor girl must have been, and of all that she must have suffered under her step-mother's treatment. His daughter steadfastly keeping her faith and simplicity in the midst of such adverse circumstances—bearing all her troubles with so much patience and amiability—made him compare her to the lotus which rears its blossom of dazzling beauty out of the slime and mud of the moats and ponds, fitting emblem of a heart which keeps itself unsullied while passing through the world.

The step-mother, anxious to know what would happen, had all this while been standing outside the room. She had grown interested, and had gradually pushed the sliding screen back till she could see all that went on. At this moment she suddenly entered the room, and dropping to the mats, she bowed her head over her outspread hands before her step-daughter.

"I am ashamed! I am ashamed!" she exclaimed in broken tones. "I did not know what a filial child you were. Through no fault of yours, but with a step-mother's jealous heart, I have disliked you all the time. Hating you so much myself, it was but natural that I should think you reciprocated the feeling, and thus when I saw you retire so often to your room I followed you, and when I saw you gaze daily into the mirror for long intervals, I concluded that you had found out how I disliked you, and that you were out of revenge trying to take my life by magic art. As long as I live I shall never forget the wrong I have done you in so misjudging you, and in causing your father to suspect you. From this day I throw away my old and wicked heart, and in its place I put a new one, clean and full of repentance. I shall think of you as a child that I have borne myself. I shall love and cherish you with all my heart, and thus try to make up for all the unhappiness I have caused you. Therefore, please throw into the water all that has gone before, and give me, I beg of you, some of the filial love that you have hitherto given to your own lost mother."

Thus did the unkind step-mother humble herself and ask forgiveness of the girl she had so wronged.

Such was the sweetness of the girl's disposition that she willingly forgave her step-mother, and never bore a moment's resentment or malice towards her afterwards. The father saw by his wife's face that she was truly sorry for the past, and was greatly relieved to see the terrible misunderstanding wiped out of remembrance by both the wrong-doer and the wronged.

From this time on, the three lived together as happily as fish in water. No such trouble ever darkened the home again, and the young girl gradually forgot that year of unhappiness in the tender love and care that her step-mother now bestowed on her. Her patience and goodness were rewarded at last.

A NOTE ON THE SOURCES

———

These stories come from two collections published in the early 20th century. Lafcadio Hearn (1850–1904), the author of *Kwaidan*, was born in Greece and lived in Ireland and the United States before he settled in Japan and became a naturalized citizen. For his book, he recorded tales from oral storytellers and translated existing written versions. Yei Theodora Ozaki (1871–1932), the author of *Japanese Fairy Tales*, was half Japanese, half English and lived most of her life in Japan. For her collection, she translated stories by Sadanami Sanjin and Shinsui Tamenaga, as well as a story from the classic work *Taketori Monogatari*. The tales in this book have been excerpted from the following editions of *Kwaidan* and *Japanese Fairy Tales*, both of which are in the public domain:

Hearn, Lafcadio. *Kwaidan: Stories and Studies of Strange Things*. Reprint of the Houghton Mifflin Company 1911 Boston and New York edition, Internet Archive, 2013. https://archive.org/details/kwaidanstoriesst00hear

Ozaki, Yei Theodora. *Japanese Fairy Tales*. Reprint of the Grosset & Dunlap 1908 New York edition, Internet Archive, 2007. https://archive.org/details/japanesefairytal00ozak

SOURCES

The Dream of Akinosuké
From *Kwaidan*, by Lafcadio Hearn

The Jelly Fish and the Monkey
From *Japanese Fairy Tales*,
by Yei Theodora Ozaki

Momotaro, or the Story
of the Son of a Peach
From *Japanese Fairy Tales*,
by Yei Theodora Ozaki

The Happy Hunter
and the Skillful Fisher
From *Japanese Fairy Tales*,
by Yei Theodora Ozaki

The Bamboo-Cutter and the
Moon-Child
From *Japanese Fairy Tales*,
by Yei Theodora Ozaki

The Story of Mimi-Nashi-Hōïchi
From *Kwaidan*, by Lafcadio Hearn

Yuki-Onna
From *Kwaidan*, by Lafcadio Hearn

Diplomacy
From *Kwaidan*, by Lafcadio Hearn

Mujina
From *Kwaidan*, by Lafcadio Hearn

A Dead Secret
From *Kwaidan*, by Lafcadio Hearn

Rokuro-Kubi
From *Kwaidan*, by Lafcadio Hearn

The Tongue-Cut Sparrow
From *Japanese Fairy Tales*,
by Yei Theodora Ozaki

The Farmer and the Badger
From *Japanese Fairy Tales*,
by Yei Theodora Ozaki

The Story of the Old Man Who
Made Withered Trees to Flower
From *Japanese Fairy Tales*,
by Yei Theodora Ozaki

The Mirror of Matsuyama:
A Story of Old Japan
From *Japanese Fairy Tales*,
by Yei Theodora Ozaki